THE RESURRECTION OF ARGENT

Land of Jonrah Series

Book 2

C.S. Zahn

ISBN: 9781962973526

DEDICATION

This book, and future books of this series, is dedicated to our cat Eevee who passed away on Monday, October 16, 2016, at 7:50 pm. She was diagnosed with mammary cancer in March 2016. She had surgery and it was found to have spread into her lymph nodes. We started her on immunotherapy. Not sure how much this helped. The veterinarian said she would last six to eight months. She made it to seven. She passed shortly after we had moved to Vermont.

Although she is gone from this world, she will love on in these books. We miss her very much.

The land of Jonrah
Due West
Satans Kingdom
Slippery Rock
Nameless
Welcome
Argent
Fearnot
Paradise
Burnt Tree
Ghoul Creek

TABLE OF CONTENTS

PROLOGUE

WFLA_TV Tampa Channel 3 Evening News bulletin Sophia Ivanova reporting
Lake Wales, Florida, November 16, 2016

TERROR FROM BELOW | PART 2

Some of our viewers may remember the story of the Lake Wales sinkhole that engulfed the home of Alecyn Johnsenn six months ago. The story has taken on a bizarre twist since we were last here. Authorities allowed residents of Ridge Manor Drive to return to their homes after evacuating them because of safety concerns. No sooner had the United States Geological Survey deemed it safe for them to return to their home than residents began reporting lights and strange sounds coming from the enormous pit that had once been Miss Johnsenn's home. Allen Livingston, whose property is next door to the sinkhole, told us: "The entire area is boarded up. You cannot get near it. Yet, during a particular night, I found myself walking the dog and noticed light emitting from it. It was a very subtle quality. I saw things. And I thought I heard music. Maybe some kids had gotten in and were having a party. I just thought, how dumb can you be? And I called the sheriff's office. But when the police ventured inside the fenced-off area, they found nothing. No proof indicated that anyone had entered following the erection of the fences. However, residents continued reporting noises, lights, and music from the sinkhole. Ellen Jones, another neighbor, told us this. "And once, I thought I heard a flute playing. Alecyn played an Irish flute. I know that sounds crazy, but that is what it sounded like, and the sound was clear. I was unable to discern the song, even though it had a faint sense of familiarity. I don't know what it all means, but I don't think this is a natural phenomenon. I pray for poor Alecyn."

In a dark twist to this surreal tale, authorities called upon a mountain rescue team from Boulder, Colorado, to assist in the search and rescue. They went into the sinkhole, and no one has seen them since. As I speak, the residents of Manor Ridge Drive have once again evacuated their homes. Many are now seeking legal representation for a class action suit against the developer who built the homes here, claiming that this ground is unsafe. Florida's state governor is supporting their cause and demanding compensation from the federal government.

Meanwhile, Ridge Manor Drive, Lake Wales, Florida, is taking its place alongside the Bermuda Triangle and Area 51, one place shrouded in mystery that we may never understand. Of course, we will bring you more as we have it.

CHAPTER I:
HONORED GUEST

She opened her eyes to stare at the ceiling, a scream caught in her throat. She kicked off her blankets in the middle of the night. For a moment, the dream held her in its grip. She found herself back at home, with her father still alive. It had seemed so normal, waking her from downstairs, calling her for breakfast. She had gotten up. Eevee was sunning herself on the windowsill. In the kitchen, her father made his famous eggs while Jerad sat, tousled-haired and barefoot, at the kitchen table, poring over a map of the Southlands. The two men had been discussing military strategy deep in conversation, and neither had noticed the dark figure standing beyond the kitchen door watching them. Alecyn had tried to warn them. But then she heard the familiar ticking growl from behind her. She had time for one scream before the Mute attacked her. The breaking of glass followed the screams of the men as more Mutes invaded the house. The dream ended with the creature's faceplate opening.

"Bad dreams again, child?" Eevee stood in the doorway of Alecyn's room. She is shorter than Alecyn but has bright white hair and even brighter green eyes. She crossed to Alecyn, sitting on the bed.

"I heard you muttering and tossing in your bed last night. Fantasizing about your new man?" Eevee had a wicked smile, and Alecyn almost laughed aloud in relief.

"Nothing like that."

"Why not? He is a handsome devil."

"I think he resents being forced to stay here when he wants to go home to help his people."

"That is not your fault. Besides, he needs to wait if he wants a Nelim army at his back. Erevar has been speaking to as many of the clan chiefs as he can reach, but it takes time."

Eevee wasn't just a cat any longer. Her passage through the gateway to Jonrah had transformed her. In the Heart, where the rules governing the material world were more malleable, she adopted any form she wished. In this place, she appeared human. She embodied the characteristics of a cat, and she also had another attribute. She put her arm around Alecyn's shoulders, and Alecyn cuddled her, tucking her feet under her.

"Sometimes I miss your fur," Alecyn said. Eevee snorted.

"I don't miss the fur balls."

The room that they occupied resided in a small cottage that they shared.

The Nelim favored greens and blues for the decoration, and everything in it had curved lines with no straight lines anywhere. Bare, but somehow comfortable. Jerad had taken rooms with the Nelim warriors, who lived in a compound at the foot of the Great Trees. An entire town existed in and amongst root systems the size of hills. Alecyn had learned a lot about the Nelim since entering The Heart. She knew of the Canopy caste to which Erevar, and his clerics belonged and the Ground caste to which the warriors belonged. She also knew the Nelim clans were scattered everywhere except for those gathered here. They waited there to discover if Erevar could persuade those clans to join the fight against Atramen. Then, she and Jerad could come to the aid of the Southlands.

Her thoughts returned to Jerad as they did every day. It completely made sense to live separately. When they first arrived in the Heart, they all had rooms in Erevar's house. Jerad had been in the room next to Alecyn and Eevee, and she had become accustomed to seeing him every morning and saying goodnight to him each night. They had numerous discussions during the early days when they were both exploring a foreign land. But then Jerad became more distant. He spent his days training with the warriors or speaking to scouts who had ventured into the world. Not for the first time, she wondered what had changed.

Alecyn made a face. "Do you trust Erevar?" she asked suddenly. It earned her a direct look from Eevee.

"No, of course not, child. And neither should you. Erevar will have an agenda that may not be the same as ours. He opposes the Silence, which might mean our interests converge for a time. He may treat us like honored guests, but have you tried to reach the Canopy unless one of your teachers has summoned you?" Eevee's white eyebrow arched against her dark skin. "I have been polite but refused entry. The Canopy caste does not allow just anyone from Below, as they call it, entry into their domain." Eevee gave an enigmatic smile. "Fortunately, my feline form is a lot less noticeable."

"Come on." Eevee continued. "Erevar will expect you're training soon."

Alecyn did not reply. Through the open window of her room, she saw figures passing along the path that skirted the garden. She had seen Jerad pass by carrying a sheathed sword with a spear and shield on his back. She desperately wished for him to glance around at her as he passed, but his eyes remained fixated on the path.

"I don't know why that man is still here. He frets over what is happening in the Southlands." Eevee commented.

"I know. And I should help him. It is my fault they are in danger." Atramen had belonged to the Higher Hundred group, showcasing his exceptional singing prowess.

"Pish.," Eevee said dismissively. "Atramen would have reached out for the Southlands eventually if only to build up his armies."

"But he is looking for me. And he will tear apart every community to find me. And I am here, unharmed, while people are dying."

"Are we back on this again, girl? What benefits would you bring about without proper control over your powers? Atramen belonged to the Higher Hundred, signifying that he was a Singer of the greatest power.

Alecyn was unable to provide her with an answer, but it did not matter. She had been in the Heart for a month, learning about the magic of Jonrah, which she possessed herself. She couldn't deny the fascination, but the power was truly terrifying. Amid it all, there existed a sense of frustrated immobility.

The Heart is a haven, separate from and untouchable from the world outside, the perfect place for her to learn her powers. Every day, she thought of the suffering being inflicted because of her.

"Patience, Alecyn.," Eevee said soothingly. "Learn all that the Nelim can teach you. Besides, Jerad needs every warrior Erevar can give him. And for that, we need to wait. Atramen belonged to the

Higher Hundred and possessed the title of a Singer with the greatest power."

"Sometimes, I think he wants to keep us here—keep me here anyway—that he does not care about the Southlands at all."

Alecyn's eyes fell on the book, which had fallen from her bed as she had thrashed in her nightmare. Eevee followed her gaze and bent to pick it up.

"Have you read much of it?"

"As much as I can. I am always exhausted after a day of training." Alecyn told her.

"Erevar sent someone to help you, didn't he?"

"Yes, but his answers sometimes make no more sense than the book. It is all so cryptic, and he has been studying it for so long that it is like he has lost the ability to speak plainly. Sometimes, I think they are all trying to steer me in a particular direction and keep me from anything that might help me decide." The euphoria of finally finding a safe place in Jonrah, where she did not have to be afraid, had given way to a wariness that grew with each passing day.

"Let me look into it for you," Eevee said, squeezing her shoulder. "As Eevee the cat, I can reach the highest levels of the Canopy and ask some questions of the Trees themselves."

"They won't stop you?"

"They won't see me, then." Eevee admonished. "I told you, Eevee the cat is far harder to spot than Eevee the... other."

CHAPTER 2:
IN SONG

Alecyn sat cross-legged on a bed of blue-green moss. She wore the clothes of a Nelim apprentice Singer, a pale blue tunic with baggy trousers and cinched at the ankle. She walked barefoot in the Heart, as did the Nelim. They sat high in the canopy of the Great Trees. The ground was a dizzying distance far below. Around them, an ocean of trees on the scale of mountains. Between the huge trunks, she caught glimpses of green hills in the distance. The interlocking branches that formed the canopy above them shut out the sunlit sky but made up for this with thousands of lights on the underside of the branches.

Opposite her sat Erevar, similarly cross-legged. Alecyn followed the instructions, which were the first she had learned, clearing her mind by humming a tune to herself, a simple phrase from a handful of notes. She repeated it until her worries, thoughts about Jerad, and doubts about Erevar subdued. Her muscles relaxed. She did not realize she had been so tense. Her breathing slowed and deepened. And at the edge of her awareness appeared the symphony of life all around them.

"Good." came Erevar's voice, adopting a sing-song tone. "Your song has become a serene melody, reaching beyond you to affect the world around you. But that is an unconscious effect. Like music, spillage spreads out in all directions and is heard by many beyond its intended audience. We are here to learn to control it and direct it. Use it. So, tell me of the Three Orders of Music."

Alecyn repeated. "Song is the highest order, for it manifests the will. The instrument is the second and the most common. Many can work magical effects on an instrument, but the power is less than the music of the object, not the person. Noise is the third. It is the most destructive and the easiest to produce."

As Erevar nodded approvingly and gestured for her to continue, Alecyn recited the lessons she had learned from Erevar and the other clerics who had taught her. Some walked her through magical exercises, moving objects, healing damaged parts of the trees, and defending herself from attacks. Other lessons concerned the theory of magic and the sources of magical power, the World, the Self, and others. Erevar regarded using any power but that of the Self as a great evil.

"Take from the World or Others", and it will take away your Song, erode it to nothing. You will become like Kragen Onyx, you will be Silent."

"But I don't understand. How is he Silent? How does he have no Song?"

"It got lost long, long ago. He survived. But for a mortal being such as a human to live without a song?" Erevar shook his head sadly. "It can only be an existence of torment."

"What is it he wants?"

"Control of the Great Song."

"How?"

Erevar had spread his long-fingered hands, lifting his shoulders. "Who can fathom the purposes of such as he? No other being in this world has ever been like him. Even his lieutenants are years away from the level of degradation he has reached."

Alecyn suddenly noticed a change in the music she perceived all around her. It was the song of the Nelim mystic opposite her, shifting in melody and pitch. She had learned to read those auras that everyone had, the Song, a manifestation of their soul. She had touched those auras and altered them to heal. And now she was able to discern that Erevar was lying.

"Are you hiding something from me, Erevar?" she said, refusing to look away from the blue-eyed stare that came back to her.

"You are learning, child. Very well done. I did not even sense your reading of me."

"Are you?" Alecyn refused to be diverted. She focused her awareness on Erevar's Song but could feel resistance. It shifted in and out of hearing as though coming from a radio station being tuned in and out. Erevar shielded himself from her.

"Of course, I am. There are many things I know you cannot do. Which you are not ready to know."

"About Kragen Onyx. About the prophecy?"

"Particularly about those subjects. I will tell you what you need to know to realize your potential. I withhold nothing that might prevent you from defeating Kragen Onyx." Regarding the prophecy, Erevar steered the conversation back to Alecyn's lessons. She followed his instructions, but her suspicions remained.

CHAPTER 3:
TRAVEL BY LEAF

Alecyn descended through the layers of Canopy atop a giant leaf. The method of travel was commonly chosen by those who wanted to descend to the ground. By whistling a simple tune, Alecyn detached the leaves and controlled them when summoned. It had been terrifying at first, but now she was able to control the airflow that held the leaf aloft while only half thinking about it. It spun, glided, bobbed, and weaved in amongst the giant, ever-lower trunks. Around her, she saw others ascending and descending through the dimming light. The night drew in, and the Canopy lights from the interlocking branches above dimmed, fading to faint oranges and blues even as the sky beyond dimmed.

She heard something buzzing. She was so startled that she almost lost control of the airflow and pitched herself off the leaf entirely. The buzz repeated, followed by a tinkling tune coming from the inside pocket of her tunic. Alecyn quickly realized it came from her phone!

She carried it with her as a reminder of home, a comfort in a strange place, though it had been dark and dead since she had arrived in Jonrah. She tore at the lacings of her tunic and reached into the pocket sewn into the inner lining. A bright artificial light shone through the material in a rectangular shape.

Her fingers trembled as she took out the phone while cycling through its startup screens. She clutched it in two hands as she stared at it. It seemed to be working! She tapped at the phone symbol on the home screen and briefly saw her contacts list flash up before the screen went dark. She pressed the power button, then the volume button, and the sleep button. Then, combinations of all three. She stabbed and swiped at the now dark glass, increasingly desperate. Tears filled her eyes, and she spoke aloud.

"No! No! No! No! Come back! Come back! Please!"

Her hair whipped around her head, and she realized that the air current carrying her had strengthened into a gale. The roaring slipstream that engulfed Alecyn buffeted other leaves, causing their riders to fight to control their flight as they passed nearby. All thought left her as she fell to her knees on the soft, yielding surface, still staring at the phone. She hurtled towards the underside of a branch and, with a scream, instinctively changed the airflow. The leaf plummeted after passing a hair's breadth from dashing her against the tree. It cannoned into a tree trunk, hurling her full length, the phone flying from her hand towards the edge. She scrambled after it and caught it, only to lose her grip following another impact. She caught it again, but the leaf tipped, and she was sliding off. The ground sped towards her but remained distant enough to break every bone in her body. Holding the phone in a white-knuckled grip, she forced her awareness to narrow around it. She could feel the smooth plastic digging into her fingers. A calmness flooded her, and she sang a thrilling series of wordless notes. The leaf flipped on a sudden buffeting of air, and Alecyn found herself hurled skyward to land on the now-level surface with a thump. It continued its descent more calmly until it landed gently on the ground. Alecyn's knees trembled so much that she didn't think she could stand.

She became aware of Nelim figures running towards her. Roots towered around her, spotted with the openings of windows and doors. Then, a familiar voice.

"Alecyn! Are you OK?"

Only one person in the Heart knew that expression, coming as it did from her world, not Jonrah. It was Jerad. He was on the leaf with her. He had bare arms, and his hair was clumped with sweat. Concern twisted his features, and his eyes never left her. The trembling had spread now through the rest of her body as the adrenalin took over. She tried to speak. Then Jerad embraced her tightly, lifting her off the ground. Awash in Jerad's Song, it engulfed her, flooding her awareness completely. Strident fear and panic threaded the music, dominating his theme. She touched it instinctively, soothing it. Then Jerad wrapped his arms around her and picked her up. His Song was heroic, anthemic, and strong, and her head slumped against his chest as she allowed it to suffuse her.

"Alecyn?" The voice was gentle and warm. "Can you hear me? It's Jerad."

"I know," Alecyn whispered with eyes closed. "I'm ok." She opened her eyes, and his face was her world. It carried bruises, evidence of the hard training he put himself through. She sensed the imperfections in his Song that indicated those minor hurts. The tones were off, and she corrected them easily. The bruises vanished, and she saw the recognition in his eyes. Then, a smile that she couldn't help but return.

"Would it not be polite to ask before doing that?" He chided gently.

"Probably. I can't seem to help it."

"What happened to you, Alecyn? I saw the leaf falling. I didn't realize it was you until I got closer. I thought... I thought you were..."

Alecyn didn't need to read Jerad to see the emotion, and it triggered warm feelings within her. Then she remembered.

"My phone! My phone!" It was not in her hand or pocket. She looked about herself in a sudden panic. "Where is it?"

"Is this what you're looking for?" Jerad handed it to her. "You dropped it on the leaf. What is it?"

"It's my phone!" Alecyn supplied without really thinking that Jerad wouldn't understand the word. "It's a device." She explained. "For talking over great distances. But it hasn't worked since I arrived here."

"In the Heart?"

"No, in Jonrah. It has been completely dead. But up there, it came to life, just for a second. Jerad, it came back to life!"

She saw the confusion on his face, which seemed to mirror her own.

"I don't know how or even what it means, but it happened. It must mean something!"

Jerad nodded, clearly not understanding but knowing that something significant had occurred. He had shifted away from her as she sat up and let his arms drop until his hand on her arm was the only contact.

"You're unhurt?" He asked.

"I think so. I must find Eevee, though. See if she can make sense of this."

She was dimly aware that Jerad's Song was losing its volume, dimming, and growing softer. He looked down at the arm he touched and deliberately took away his hand, his fingertips lingering for a heartbeat.

He stood abruptly. "I haven't seen her for a few days. Both of you. I don't know where she is."

Alecyn looked at him and climbed to her feet, tucking the phone back into her pocket.

"I have been busy with training. Erevar is pushing me hard to learn all I can before the clans arrive and we leave."

"Do you know when that will be?" Jerad's eyes did not meet hers, and his words and tone were stiff. "The Highs are not providing us with any information."

"I don't. I am sorry. Erevar only talks about what I need to learn. And tells me to be patient. I'm sorry, Jerad. I will try to push him. I know you want to go home. So do I."

Jerad looked at her, and she stammered. "I mean... I want to go with you... to help. I want to do whatever I can to help". She thought he looked handsome when he smiled and blushed, looking away. She missed his smile. When he spoke again, there was a formality to his words.

"If you can, I would be grateful. I am no longer allowed into the Canopy and have been unable to speak to Erevar. Anything you can do, please do."

"I will. I promise."

"Good. Well, I must go. Vanja's patrol is due back anytime now, and I would like to know what he's found."

She mumbled something in reply as he was striding away from her. He didn't glance back, though she kept her eyes on him until he vanished from sight among a group of warriors.

CHAPTER 4:
TRAINING WITH THE NELIM

Jerad wondered if he was about to die again. He had suffered death seven times before in this arena. That was a benefit of being in a realm in which the physical was purely an illusion; combat training was for real. The thought skittered over the periphery of his awareness and was gone. In place of the thought, the warrior's focus remained. He became more aware of his surroundings. He felt gritty, slightly loose soil under his boots, sweat dripping from his temple, the leather-wrapped hilt in his hand, and the slightest movement of the purple-skinned killer in front of him.

Vanja was the leader of the Heart's warriors. His wiry torso was bare, his purple skin darkened by elaborate tattoos. Two long, multi-jointed limbs extended from his back, over his shoulder and vanished into five-foot lengths of sharpened steel. Unlike other Nelim, his head was bald, with a crawling mass of intricate dark lines crisscrossing his scalp. His eyes were bright indigo, and his face was long, thin, and hard. He wore the traditional green and blue patterned kilt here in the Heart. The standard attire of the warriors. At least, that was the appearance he imagined for himself here. Jerad had to keep reminding himself that this place was not material. It was a construct somewhere beyond the real world. In the Heart, they created their physical forms.

Erevar had tried to explain over dinner early in their stay, but Jerad's mind had reeled, and he had nodded politely, smiled, and sat back. Magic had always been beyond him, even when Alyssa had been alive. Alecyn and Eevee had spent long hours talking with Erevar; he supposed it was only natural, but it further cemented his feelings of distance. He had seen Alecyn safely there. There was no reason for him to stay.

A line of fire scored his chest as Vanja's blade sliced through him. A shout rang out from the sidelines of the stone circle where they dueled, showing a hit. Jerad's reactions were instinctive; he fluidly parried and blocked the next three blows that rained down on him and put himself beyond the Nelim's reach. He plucked a knife from his belt and flicked it out underhand. Vanja hissed as the blade thudded into his shoulder. Two shouts rang out from the opposite side of the circle, then a resounding gong. Jerad never took his eyes off Vanja's as the healing was sung out over them. The Nelim's stare as sharp as his blades. Their respective wounds closed, blood drying and flaking away from sudden whole skin. Only the fatigue remained. The duel continued.

Around them, Vanja's company sat cross-legged, watching the fight, purple and blue eyes watching each move keenly. Some held sticks in which they scrawled in the dirt pictures of weaknesses noted in the combatant's movements and shared with those around them. Recognized tactics being displayed and new ones being discovered. Others shouted encouragement or roars of approval for a good attack or defense. Around them, an intricate maze of twisting branches and trunks formed a circular structure open to the sky. The twisted mass of tree life formed screens behind which were rooms and passageways. The Nelim could stride through the maze and see it change about their person. Engulfing one to take him to a higher story. Opening before another to the forest grove of larger trees surrounding the building. Jerad couldn't make the architecture move. He needed to be invited into this inner sanctum and escorted from it. This was the temple of Ranis, the last surviving god of the Nelim, the god of war. Here, Jerad had found somewhere he belonged. While trapped in the sylvan limbo of the Heart, he rediscovered the martial arts that had once made him so dangerous. By doing so, he could make a positive impact once he joined the battle against Atramen.

Vanja moved forelimbs, thrusting forward while the hind limbs arced apart and came scything together on either side of Jerad's head. It was a standard four-armed Nelim attack, and Jerad had learned how to defend against it after his seventh 'death' in this arena. Choosing a side, he brought his blade up to block the hind limb while stepping aside and twisting his body to avoid the frontal thrust. He lashed out with one foot at Vanja's wrist while striking with his elbow towards the Nelim's face. The boot struck home, but Vanja used the momentum and twisted his upper body away from the blow that would have left him blinded by his own blood. He hammered down with one hind limb, and Jerad dropped to a knee, crossing his own blades to catch the strike. Then he rolled, heaving upwards with the last of his strength to throw Vanja's blades up and swinging his own low to cut the Nelim's legs from under him.

His sword cut into flesh and bone, and he heard the Nelim scream. His own legs gave way beneath him as he underestimated the reach of those hind limbs, and one of Vanja's blades speared his thigh.

There were two shouts from both sides of the circle and another gong. The Song of Healing floated through the air, but Jerad knew his limitations. He threw down his sword and called out words in the Nelim tongue.

"Varsha! Varsha!"

It meant 'enough,' and it was the sign that he was withdrawing from the combat. A smattering of applause came from the warriors around the circle, most of whom Jerad had sparred or fought against. A rolling clash of gongs showed a break in the fighting. Vanja approached the adjudicator seated on either side of the circle and spoke briefly before leaving. He ignored the hand Jerad offered, not looking back at his opponent. Jerad stood for a moment, watching the towering warrior. He had made friends amongst the warrior Nelim, but Vanja had been openly hostile from the beginning. Many of Vanja's combats against Nelim's opponents went to death. All his battles with Jerad had done so. Jerad walked back to his place in the circle.

"Never mind, Thundercloud," a Nelim warrior named Hath said. "He is the purest of all of us. Ranis' way is that battle is the only way to prepare for battle. Here in the Heart, we can kill each other a hundred times."

"He seems keen to kill me," Jerad replied. The circle was breaking up, warriors milled, discussing the combat they had seen or participated in.

"I noticed." Hath frowned. "I cannot explain this. Speaking to the one you kill in the arena afterward is good manners. It is too easy for a bad tune to build up otherwise between us. But I am not the only one who noticed his lack of courtesy."

He pointed, and Jerad saw one of the combat adjudicators remonstrating Vanja. As they did, Jerad faced a barrage of looks and gestures from Vanja. In a posture of aggression, Vanja raised both of his hind limbs. A warrior beside Hath, whose skin was sky blue and crisscrossed with scars, made a disgusting sound.

"Vanja has no respect. It is not right to speak to an official of the temple like that!

"Will you tell him that, Ulfen?" asked another.

"Perhaps if ten of us tell him, one of us may live to finish the sentence?" said another. Jerad thought his name was Ollen.

"Make that twenty!" someone called out.

Suddenly, Vanja looked over at Jerad and then strode towards him. Jerad suppressed the urge to reach for his sword. He continued calmly, drying the sweat from his body with his shirt and did not look away.

"The Adjudicator accuses me of dishonorable conduct. I will not have my name slurred, so I wish all here to know. You are a liar!" Vanja barked.

Jerad stopped moving. His shirt was still scrunched against his chest. His tone was quiet, and he wasted no energy on histrionics.

"I am not."

"Liar! You ride out on our patrols! You see the devastation Atramen is visiting your homeland. And here you sit! Safe behind the magic of the Nelim."

Jerad took a step forward, staring up at the Nelim with murder in his eyes. He concealed a dagger from a sheaf at his belt in his hand, and his forearm quivered with the control needed not to stab Vanja through the heart.

"You know why I am still here, Vanja…."

"To protect your sorceress? It is she who protects you! Even inside the Heart, my skills are useless. It is the magic of the Canopy dwellers that protects us here…"

Jerad raised his voice and rode over Vanja's angry words. "I am here until Erevar can gather the clans to join the fight. I am here to bring Nelim warriors to help my people."

He looked around unexpectedly at the rumbles of discontent from those present. He saw faces harden. Hath shook his head, lips curling back. Jerad was confused, and Vanja breathed hard, rage ruling his features.

"Liar! Condemned out of your own mouth, human!"

"There are no clans outside the Heart. Not anymore!" This was the Adjudicator who had remonstrated with Vanja.

"Those who did not join the Heart were wiped out. Only a handful of caravans remain constantly moving to avoid humans, Kajani, or The Silence."

Jerad was stunned. "But Erevar told us. He said it would take time to gather the clan leaders. That he would speak to them to raise an army!" He stepped back from the confrontation with Vanja, turning away. He had been here, waiting for weeks.

"He even told us that Harlmen of the Kavashi and Rillan of the Narketh had agreed and that he was seeking the others."

Silence fell over the warriors, who now looked at each other, frowning. The warriors whispered the names Jerad had spoken back and forth. Vanja spoke, his tone quieter.

"The Kavashi are no more human. I stood with the last of their clan and saw him die at the gates of the Skylands."

"Did Erevar counsel you to keep silent about these clan chiefs?" asked the other Adjudicator, a rotund Nelim called Varelus. He was shorter than Jerad but deadly in unarmed combat. Vanja's darting of his head to him mirrored Jerad's own. Both minds leaped ahead to the root of that question.

"He did," Jerad replied flatly.

"There was a Song feud between the Pirus and the Kavashi, was there, not Vanja?" Varelus asked.

Vanja nodded, his intense blue-eyed stare returning to Jerad.

"Perhaps he told you mentioning them would stir up trouble in the Temple?" Varelus asked Jerad.

"He did," Jerad replied. "And so, I guarantee I will not expose his lie."

He finished, and Vanja nodded.

"Canopy scum!" someone shouted in a sudden rage. Many throats echoed the sentiment. The air filled with the clicking sound as multiple joints flexed, accompanying the unsheathing of hind limbs.

"I am no liar, Vanja. I have given my body to the Code, my life. I did this to strike a blow at our common enemy. The path to glory is bloody." He quoted the words repeated reverently by those gathered. Vanja reached up automatically to touch the tips of his hind limbs, as did all, a tribute to the god of war who had changed the bodies of the warrior caste to make them better able to honor the martial code. Jerad responded in kind, clasping his hands together before his face.

A rage had ignited within him, but he held it in careful check. It had been long since that anger had ruled him, and he was not yet ready to let it rule him again. Erevar had lied to keep him away from his people in the Heart. Why? Because he wanted Alecyn to stay. Would she even leave if Jerad did? When they arrived, circumstances had thrown them together. They had talked and spent hours in each other's company as comfort against the alienness of where they found themselves.

But Jerad had ended that closeness by leaving the house they had all three shared. Left when he realized his feelings for Alecyn.

He pulled his shirt over his head. "I need to talk to Erevar. Hath, would you show me the way out?"

Vanja caught his arm as he turned away. "I will guide you out, human."

While still rumbling, the crowds separated. The Adjudicators were leaving in the opposite direction, heads together. The thin, interwoven branches that comprised the temple fabric parted before the tall warrior and Jerad followed. Beyond the temple was a wide clearing of short grass surrounded by towering trees, their tops lost to sight high above.

"It troubles me that Erevar would lie in this way," Vanja said, leading Jerad across the clearing to a cluster of long-legged animals tethered to stakes in the ground. They had long necks covered in thick grey fur and were grazing on the grass. A few looked up at the approaching figures, and Jerad saw multiple limbs briefly flexing out from the creature's flanks. He had a sinking feeling.

"He's made it clear to us that Alecyn should learn her craft."

"That would take a long time, would it not?" Vanja asked.

"I imagine so."

"And how long could your Southlands stand against Atramen?"

"If people gather instead of trying to fight separately, in Fearnot or Ghoul's Creek, they could hold out for a few months."

"So, likely, Erevar means to abandon the Southlands."

Jerad nodded grimly.

"And we would miss our chance to fight our enemy."

They had reached the nearest of the tethered creatures, and Jerad saw that each had saddles strapped to their backs.

"Have you ridden a Treewalker before, human?"

"No. And my name is Jerad," he replied pointedly.

Vanja nodded his head briefly in assent. "You will find the experience disturbing, then. But it is the fastest way to travel in the Canopy. For you, anyway. Follow."

Vanja deftly mounted the saddle with four indentations for riders, stretching down the creature's long back to its tail. Jerad climbed into a seat behind Vanja and gripped a rope ring attached to it. At a command from Vanja, four limbs unfolded from either side of the creature's back, and it stood. Then, with a single bound, it leaped for the nearest tree, gripping the bark with claws in its powerful hind limbs and propelling itself upwards. Jerad stared vertically skywards, aware of the increasing drop beneath them. He knew he could not die here, but he couldn't suppress the fear of falling.

"Treewalkers are extinct in the world now," Vanja commented easily, unaware of the drop. "They exist only in the Heart. They are another relic of the past the Canopy surrounds themselves with, blocking out the present."

Jerad suppressed a yelp as the Treewalker launched away from the tree, twisting in the air so its passengers were not upside down. Its glide took it up and then down in a graceful curve, which suddenly ended when its hind limbs shot out to grasp at a branch above. Jerad felt his breath being jerked out of him and then again as the creature hauled itself upwards and through the air again, only to slam to a halt as it caught another branch. By this means, it worked its way higher until finally settling on a broad wooden platform.

"Where are we?" Jerad asked, trying to hide the shakiness in his knees as he dismounted.

"This is the Concourse, the gateway to the Canopy."

"I have tried to enter before now to speak to Erevar. They do not allow me entry."

"I am the leader of the Velesten and a ruling council member; I sit on the ruling council. No one can refuse me.

Vanja strode across the platform towards tall wooden gates. Jerad saw stairs cut into and through the body of a massive tree. Walkers glided and grabbed through the surrounding air. Despite the crowded concourse, people made way for Vanja and Jerad. Some wore the commonplace tunics, hose, and boots at Ground level. Others wore the robes of the Canopy. The gates were a tight woven mesh of vines that parted for those in Canopy dress or at a gesture from an orderly seated cross-legged on large cushions. Those in Groundling dress waited patiently to speak to the orderly and gain entry.

Vanja did not wait in line. He strode to the nearest orderly, standing close enough that the Nelim had to crane his neck to look up.

"I am Vanja kaPirus, Sankari of the Velesten and member of the High Council."

The orderly appeared unfazed by Vanja's attempts at intimidation. "And your companion?"

"You know who he is as well as I! The entire Heart knows by now of the humans we shelter. We require entry to speak to Erevar on an urgent matter."

"And what would that matter be, Sankari?"

"Our matter."

The Nelim sighed exaggeratedly. "Sankari, despite your rank, you are not given automatic access to the Canopy, which is not the province of the Groundborn. I am instructed…"

He didn't finish his speech as Vanja plucked him from his seat, holding him to eye level. "Allow us entry, or I will send you to the Groundborn by the most direct route possible."

"I cannot!" the orderly spluttered. "Erevar has ordered that the human male not be allowed entry."

"Me then," Vanja answered.

"Nor any of the Velesten. I am sorry, I cannot."

The orderly's eyes were wide and pleading. Jerad realized that the Nelim believed that Vanja might do good on this threat. He suddenly saw himself in the tall warrior, as he had been in the days following the fall of Argent. Savage, brutal, cruel. He wondered what fueled the anger that so clearly coursed through Vanja's veins. He put a restraining hand on the Nelim's arm.

"Vanja. Put him down. There is nothing we can do here."

He shifted his position to look the Nelim in the eye.

"We cannot force our way in here. Can we?" He had a feeling more than gates protected the Canopy, and Vanja's nod confirmed it. He lowered the orderly to his feet.

"This is outrageous even for you, Vanja kaPirus! Erevar will learn of this behavior and censure you for it!"

Vanja growled and turned away under Jerad's guiding hand, hind limbs tense and poised to strike. They walked away, given an even wider berth by Canopy and Groundlings.

Jerad's mind raced. Erevar was trying to keep him away from Alecyn.

Why? Was he trying to control her? To what end? He did not know enough about Erevar to guess.

"Is there another way into the Canopy?" He asked Vanja.

"No. Erevar's magic is rife here. We could take a Walker and climb higher but would find ourselves back here again. The only way to climb is through the Gates. Why do you want to go into the Canopy?"

"To speak to Alecyn or Eevee. They need to know Erevar is lying to us."

Vanja threw up his hands in disgust. "Human!"

Jerad's anger boiled over at the Nelim's high-handed manner. "What?!" he blurted. "What is it, Vanja? I understand you hating me when you thought I was a liar and a coward, but what's put a burr in your pants now?"

Vanja turned on him, their shouts drawing looks from across the Concourse. "You are as skilled a warrior as I have ever seen. You are a match for any of my Velesten, and no white skin has ever claimed that. But you find reasons to sit here on your hands. What is this female to you?"

"She is the True Voice! It is in her power to save this world!"

"Then her place is with Erevar, who can teach her to use her powers. She doesn't need you. So why are you still here?"

Jerad knew but refused to voice his feelings when he thought of Alecyn. He shook his head.

"Nothing."

Vanja smiled. He looked at them, his stare turning curious heads back to their business as it swept across the crowds. He patted Jerad's shoulder.

"Take the slow way, Groundward, Jerad. You know how to evade followers?"

Jerad nodded cursorily. "As I thought. I have business to attend but meet me at the Falls of Raurein when the Silvertops are lit. Bring everything you will need to wage war."

CHAPTER 5:
LIES

Jerad gathered the few possessions he had brought with him. He repeatedly told himself that Alecyn wouldn't even notice his absence. At this point, she had become fully immersed in the study of magic. How was it possible for a mere soldier to capture her interest? He did not hold the rank of a general or an influential leader. He had fallen into the position of Councilman in Fearnot simply by telling people what made sense. A war was going on, and he could create an impact there. So why did he think he was making the incorrect choice? He knew how to fight Mutes; he knew the terrain. His place was in battle. So why did he feel like he was making the wrong decision?

"She doesn't need me!" He muttered savagely, pulling a drawstring tight to secure his whip bow to his back. He shoved blades into sheathes behind his shield.

"Who doesn't? And what would you be doing, boy?" came Eevee's voice.

Jerad whirled, one hand reaching for the sheathed blade at his belt. Eevee sat on the windowsill, kicking her legs.

"How in the Song did you get here?" Jerad demanded.

"I jumped up."

"We are three floors up, at least," Jerad challenged.

"Nothing for a young cat, and I can be a young cat again whenever I choose. So, could you if you wanted to?"

"I don't have magic." Jerad turned back to check his equipment.

"It's not magic! It's just this." She tapped her forehead. "This whole place is conjured by the minds of those who live here. Stop seeing it as physical; you would find it easier to get yourself about."

"It's not important, anyway. I am leaving."

"And where do you think you are going without telling us? As if I need to ask!"

Jerad shrugged and made for the door. Eevee appeared in it, blocking his way. He strode towards her, but she refused to be intimidated and fixed him with a point to the chest.

"You are going out to get yourself killed!"

"I am going to do what I can. I am doing no good here!"

"Leaving the Heart without Nelim troops at your back is suicide, man! Are you an idiot?"

"Erevar lied to us!" Jerad shouted. "There are no clans outside. This is the Nelim nation. Here. A few hundred Velesten are under Vanja's command, but that is it! Understand, feline."

He tried to shoulder his way past her and regretted it. Something hit Jerad like a sledgehammer and flung him against the wall, arms splayed as though pinned to the wall. Eevee advanced with eyes blazing. Her white hair seemed to almost stand on end.

"Release me!" Jerad yelled with a raised eyebrow.

"Enough of your foolishness! This is serious. Explain what you just said!" Eevee demanded, folding her arms and fixing him with a look he had last seen on his mother's face.

"Vanja told me that the clans who stayed outside died. There are no clans out there. I went to talk to Erevar, and they barred us from entering the Canopy.

"Nonsense. Erevar would not stop you from coming in. Vanja, maybe if he were stomping about in one of his tempers. That boy would pick a fight with his own shadow."

"It's true, Eevee." Jerad let the anger go. He sighed. "I do not know what game he is playing, but he wants me apart from the two of you."

Eevee put her hand to her chin, walking up and down the passageway.

"Now, what is the blue devil up to, eh? He knows Alecyn wants to help the Southlands. And if you leave, she will want to go with you. So, he keeps you here until you see through his ruse and then separates you, so Alecyn doesn't find out you are leaving until it's too late. But then, what's stopping Alecyn and I from going off after you?"

"She wouldn't."

"Ah, hush, man. Of course, she would!"

Suddenly, Jerad dropped to the floor with a painful bump. He picked himself up amid a tangle of weapons and equipment. He glared balefully at Eevee.

"Like you said, just imagine the Heart with me standing on my feet. It's no magic at all."

Despite being taken aback, Eevee didn't show any signs of it. "Don't you be going anywhere until I've spoken to Alecyn, young man...." she began.

"Hold your tongue, feline," Jerad snapped back. "Where I am going is no place for an apprentice sorcerer or, for that matter, a woman. No, Alecyn is better off not knowing me."

Eevee opened her mouth to deliver a furious response, but Jerad kept talking.

"Now, imagine a Heart where I am exactly where I need…" he disappeared.

"A fine time you pick to unravel the mysteries of a higher dimension. Foolish man!" Eevee yelled. Then she, too, disappeared.

****

Jerad appeared beside a pool that gleamed mirror bright in the glow of the silver-topped trees. They were slim, bowled, and smooth-skinned, with leafless branches tipped with bulbous buds. Spread throughout the Heart, or at least the parts Jerad had seen. And at nighttime, they glowed silver, like moonlight. Above the pool, a waterfall cascaded furiously from stone terraces, bouncing, and hammering its way into the pool. The Velesten gathered about the pool, all in battle dress and armed. As Jerad appeared in their midst, there were alarmed shouts and the sibilant hiss of steel drawn everywhere. Vanja called his warriors back to calm down. He strode through the Nelim with a broad grin visible beneath a burnished helm.

"Well, Jerad. You are full of surprises. Using Canopy tricks to take us unawares."

"You told me to evade followers, did you not, Vanja?" Jerad replied. "Are you going to tell me what we are doing here?"

"We go to war, my friend. We merely await the hour."

Suddenly, the sound of a thousand thunderclaps filled the air. A bright white line tore across the sky in a jagged streak. At first, Jerad thought it was lightning. Then it widened, becoming brighter until it drowned out the gentle glow from the Silvertops. The sky folded away to the horizon as the white light widened further.

Jerad threw his hands against the bright light and began making out black dots against the white. They grew in size, then warped in shape, becoming black streaks moving against the white and moving downwards. He realized what he saw. Something emerged from the light and fell to the ground—a hundred-somethings.

"It's a breach!" Vanja roared. Vanja roared, declaring that someone had invaded the Heart. "Velesten to war!"

CHAPTER 6:
SCRYING PATH

Eevee reappeared in the Canopy. The power Erevar used to keep others out didn't seem to touch her, and she wondered at that. As her consciousness awakened in her feline form, so did her awareness of magic, but she did not know where that came from in her. Who was that person? She knew that her personality had elements of the cat she had been. Her arrogance was in her, and she instinctively knew it came from the cat. There was also an irascibility that contrasted with a deep affection for humans, Alecyn and Jerad especially. But she knew things that went far beyond understanding in this world. That dawned on her the longer she spent in the Heart, and she saw the extent of Erevar's powers. She could perceive beyond those powers, unraveling the heart's inner workings to its fundamental mechanics. That did not come from a cat.

She was one level up from the concourse. At this hour, the walkway she stood on was deserted as was the concourse below. The gates remained guarded, as they would be at every hour of the day and night. A glittering array of firelights peppered the surrounding night. Torches and lamps in windows and along the walkways and stairways. Treewalkers had lamps hung from their necks, and these lights bobbed and swung through the empty air between branches. She could feel Alecyn above her and felt she knew where the girl was. In the Canopy library with Mendel, the acolyte Erevar had assigned her to help translate the prophecy. During the moments when Alecyn wasn't receiving instruction from Erevar, she devoted her time to thoroughly examining the book he had given to her. Or anxiously worrying about Jerad, all the while refusing to admit it to herself.

She noticed a furtive movement down towards the Canopy gates. It was a figure clad in black, darting out of sight around the tree. Eevee felt the old feline instinct to chase but suppressed it. A spy watched her and ran off to report her re-entry into the Canopy. She had been aware of being followed, though she hadn't mentioned it to Alecyn. She smiled to herself. Let them stew about how I get in and out of the Canopy like one born to the heights!

She pictured herself in the library but then dismissed the image. There was time left yet to tell Alecyn of Jerad's foolish plan. He couldn't get far, anyway. No, she wanted to know what Erevar was up to. She smiled to herself and transformed into a cat. Let them try to follow a cat that didn't want to be followed. Padding deeper into the tree's shadow, she leaped against the bark, digging in her claws and scampering vertically before leaping to a higher branch. She flitted like a shadow higher up the tree. She stopped when she reached a small alcove, an ancient furrow in the bark deep enough to conceal her. Concealed by the deeper shadows within, she curled up, licking her fur while she focused her mind.

There was no telling where Erevar was. Her familiarity was limited to the rooms in his house he had shown them when they first arrived. It was as good a place as any to start, she supposed. Eevee disappeared from her lofty perch to reappear in the corner of a room, swathed in shadow. It was one veranda of Erevar's house.

The one that faced into a copse of trees with a path of pale stone meandering through. She kept still, green eyes surveying the room. There was no sign of Erevar, but... she could feel him. His presence had always been palpable, his power a shadow cast over everything around him. She supposed that her own abilities had the same effect. But now it was different. The sensing fainter as though over a great distance, though there was no such thing as distance here.

Her eyes kept returning to the white path of gravel that wound between the trees, just visible as a ghostly white against the inky blackness. And why did she have an unshakeable foreboding that she was about to walk that path into the impenetrable dark? I am a fool! She cursed herself. I should know when to leave well enough alone! She leaped across the room in one fluid movement and, with her tail high, followed the path into the woods.

The path twisted and turned, and the ground rose and fell. Though she had taken no turns or forks, the path was unbroken. Eevee had the impression of moving through a maze. She lost any sense of direction, even the innate homing instinct of the cat. At first, she saw nothing amongst the trees, visibility failing after a few feet. Then, off to one side was a patch of pale light. Instinct told her to lose herself among the trees on the opposite side of the path, but something told her that to stray here would be dangerous. She slung along, keeping as low to the ground as possible, ears twitching and turning, alert for any unusual sound.

She came to the patch of light and saw herself, Alecyn, Jerad, and a group of Nelim walking through a forest. As she watched Mutes attacked them. Nelim and Jerad formed a circle with Alecyn at the center. When the Mutes were dead, Alecyn tended to the wounded and then knelt beside the body of one of their attackers.

"Whatever, are you wasting your time with the thing, child?!" Eevee heard herself say in exasperated tones.

"This thing was once human. I want to see how much it has changed."

"There will be nothing of the human left, Alecyn," Jerad told her coldly.

"You're both wrong!" Alecyn said. "I can feel its song. There is something there, maybe a few notes. But it is human."

"We need to move on!" a tall Nelim said gruffly.

"Wait!" ordered Alecyn. She hummed to herself and examined the Mute closely, opening its face plate and peering inside. From her vantage point on the path, Eevee felt her stomach churn at the thought. The vision faded.

Eevee stared into the darkness thoughtfully. The tall Nelim had been Vanja. She recognized that petulant little boy's tone of his. And if they were fleeing Mutes, they must have been outside of the Heart. Had it been a vision of the future? A probable future? The words suddenly blossomed in her mind. This is a Scrying Path! Where the name came from, Eevee didn't know. But it was one she knew about. She briefly lost herself in her mind, feeling on the verge of recognition. But the dawning did not come.

She was no closer to her origins, except for this new piece of knowledge which had already been in her head, from somewhere.

So, Erevar had a Scrying Path in his back garden. Sly old devil, she thought to herself. This was no Nelim art. He had borrowed this craft from the Waeferen. She now understood her instinctive reluctance to stray from the path. If she stepped into the shadows, she would get lost in the future currents. She would not find her way out again without knowing which present she would return to. She walked on, scanning the woods with the intense concentration of a hungry predator.

She saw other visions. Some she judged entirely likely. Others less so. The vision of Kajani with human warriors riding their backs into battle. She dismissed it as an unlikely future and wondered at its location so close to the path. The pale stone pathway she followed symbolized reality, with events likely to occur near the path. The further from the vision's path, the less likely it is. The woods should have been lit as bright as day with visions. But they seemed to be few. All of them featured Alecyn. He is watching her future! Somehow, Erevar has focused this Scrying Path on Alecyn. He was trying to guide her towards his own ends, no doubt.

Ahead, she noticed a brighter light and a dark figure outlined against it. It was Erevar, standing in rapt attention before a vision that was so bright it obscured the surrounding trees completely. Eevee crept closer until she, too, could see what he saw.

A man scrambled through ruins, which had clearly once been a grand building. Cracked and soiled marble tiles, walls with ragged holes. In some places, rubble slides reduce the once grand building to ruins. Gaps on the roof let in a fine rain shower around the ends of ragged beams. He wore figure-hugging black leather streaked with dirt and dust. There was a dark, wet smears that might have been blood. A metal mask partially obscured his face. A large chunk had broken away, revealing a permanently grinning, lipless mouth and tight, parchment-like skin over prominent bones. The man kept looking over his shoulder in sharp, panicked movements. He tripped and stumbled over obstacles. Gasps of fear jerked from his skeletal mouth each time.

At first, Eevee could not see what pursued the grotesque man. Then, a series of chimes sounded, which stilled the blood in her veins. It was magic but with a timbre and tone that she had not heard for a long time. The power it held was terrifying in its scope. When have I ever experienced such might? Why did it appear once upon a time when I was familiar with magic on this scale? The building ripped apart as though by an explosion. There was no sound other than the chimes, but every stone, tile, block, joist, and beam suddenly separated from all the others. As she watched, worked stone became raw ore and rock. Cut timber became trees, and other stone blocks broke apart into unidentifiable substances that glistened in the frozen moment. Eevee would have gasped if it were a natural physical response to cats. The man stumbled as the ground beneath his feet became gravel, brick, sand, and naked soil. He fell as planned, even though the surface reverted to its natural state. He rolled down the bank of a hillock once a marbled hallway, resting on his back and staring at the figure above.

Alecyn stood there and walked unhurriedly towards him, her face dark with anger.

"This is the end for weavers of dark magic, for tyrants and torturers. Let this place return to nature as before you soiled it with your presence, Atramen!"

Atramen held up a gloved hand. "Great sorceress! I can serve you! Bind me to obedience. Surely, that is not beyond your powers. Surely, nothing can be beyond you. Please, I can be of use!"

"No!" Alecyn's voice thundered, causing Atramen's mask to crumble and fall from his face. He screamed, turning away on his hands and knees, one hand covering his face.

"You will face justice for what you have done. And then so will the so-called Great Silence. And when I have all the fragments of the Song, this world will not lose its way again. I will not allow it!"

She lifted something she held in one hand. It looked like a metal sheet, but Eevee saw an inscription shining on its surface in gold light.

Alecyn moved the fingers of her other hand along the inscription and sounds emerged. Pure notes of power. They came from the contact of her finger against the metal. Atramen rose screaming from the ground, arms, and legs taut, his leather garments falling away into dust and revealing a body that was already half a corpse.

He screamed a wail of pain and suffering that came from the depths of his soul. Then, someone set him alight. His body rose higher into the air, a blazing, screaming beacon. Eevee realized with horror that Alecyn used magic to keep him alive long after the flames had consumed his body. Kept him alive as an example. Around the exploded palace in which he had sought refuge gathered an army. Battering and blood had marked their armor. They have stained their weapons from fighting. They raised their voices, chanting and beating the air with fists.

"True Voice! True Voice!"

Their roaring rose as the vision revealed their multitude, fanatical eyes, and relentless mantra.

"Burn! Burn! Burn! Burn!"

The vision faded to darkness, and Eevee stared, horrified, into the spaces between the trees.

"A dark vision, no?" Erevar turned to her, his face shrouded in darkness. He cradled an object in his arms as though it were fragile.

"Yes," Eevee replied, not bothering to be surprised that Erevar knew she had been there. "A terrible sight."

"But one which we have considered. That the knowledge and power of the girl may outstrip us, and she may become the fruition of the prophecy. A goddess with the power to reshape this world according to her Song. And rule it as a Queen."

"Alecyn wouldn't do that. She not capable!"

"Could she not, traveler? Her power will be great when she knows how to wield it. And humans are weak. Only the Nelim have the wisdom to wield the power of the True Voice."

He walked towards her, and she saw the object in his hand glowing faintly. It looked like a stiff scroll. Its edges curled but rigid.

Eevee scampered back. Maintaining the distance between them.

"I won't allow this future to pass, Erevar." She warned.

"I know. That is why you are here, is it not, traveler?"

"Why do you keep calling me that?"

"Because I have seen through your disguise. I know what you are, what you used to be. I have seen one of your kind only once and then only briefly, long ago. But the sound of your Song is unmistakable."

Despite herself, Eevee could not help but ask. "What am I?"

"You are one of those who created this world and crafted the Great Song. You made the portals, and when humankind corrupted the Song, you escaped through them. You are a Waeferen. And there is only one reason for your return in secret."

"To protect and guide Alecyn to her destiny." Eevee finished.

"Yes, as your tool to find the Fragments of the Great Song, your weapon to destroy the usurper Kragen Onyx. But when that is done? You will be her assassin."

"No!" Eevee screamed. But memories awakened in her at his words.

"I have seen it, Waeferen!" Erevar shouted, close enough that Eevee saw the blue gleam of his eyes reflected in the glow from the object he held. He gestured with one hand, a sweeping motion, and a light sprang into being amongst the trees. Eevee refused to look, but with the speed of a striking snake, Erevar grabbed her by the scruff of her neck, lifting her and turning her towards the vision. She could neither close her eyes, change her form, or break his grasp. She looked.

Alecyn stood on a windswept cliff. She wore chain mail and armor covered in musical notation in bewildering, dense script. Her Song radiated out from her, imbuing her with an aura that lit the surrounding darkness. Behind Alecyn was a nightmarish landscape of twisted black trees. They clawed the sky with bare branches, tortuously twisted and malformed.

Walls of towering thorn bushes rose above the trees, and beyond those, a structure of black stone. It sucked the light from the sky. It was now dwarfed by the girl standing on the cliff above a raging sea. The light from her aura rose to the sky as she traced out complex lines of music from her armor.

"This is the final Song, Eevee," Alecyn said. "To cast down the power of Kragen Onyx and bring the gateways into my control. Then, the recasting of Jonrah will begin, according to my design. I will make this a world where no one suffers like I have." Her voice breaking, tears encroaching but brutally suppressed. "We are not born to pain, Eevee. We are born to love, joy, and music. And Jonrah will have that. I will banish death!"

Eevee saw the figure of a cat curled atop a rock, watching Alecyn work. It was silent and expectant.

"Nothing to say, Eevee?" Alecyn asked, turning to her, her hands never leaving their playing of the Song inscribed over her body. The cat said nothing and continued to watch. As Alecyn turned away, its shape suddenly flickered. It became a tall, dark figure looming over her, multiple limbs reaching for and around her. Then it was gone, and the cat remained, green eyes reflecting the growing nimbus around Alecyn.

Suddenly, the sky ripped apart. Where dark clouds had raced and swirled over the sea, their gyrations centered on the dark fortress behind them, now a line of pure white opened. It split apart, crisscrossing the sky in all directions, forming a mesh as bright as a hundred suns. Alecyn cried out and covered her eyes. The cat remained still.

"Eevee, what's happening!"

"The moment has arrived, Alecyn. And I am sorry, but we no longer need you." Eevee stood, and her shape changed. The feline form is gone, transformed into a shape that towers over three times Alecyn's height. It was man-shaped, but a man carved from crystal. Within the faceted surface, lines of light crawled and spun. Where the face should have been was a shape, a circle bisected horizontally into two hemispheres.

"I am sorry that it has come to this, but we are ready to reclaim our world. And now that Onyx is dead, you are the last obstacle. I am sorry, my darling girl. I love you. But my duty is to my people."

The shape glowed brightly, and all the shapes inscribed onto Alecyn's armor glowed similarly. They sang out simultaneously, the terrible, bellowing music causing Alecyn's form to vibrate. She screamed, but the destructive music from her armor drowned it out. Her face trembled so fast that it became a blur. Her screams became distorted. And then the armor fell to the ground, empty.

The crystal figure that had been Eevee fell to its knees, reaching to touch the nearest piece of the armor, head bowed. Above it, the squares that divided the sky lit up, and shapes descended towards the ground.

Eevee went limp in Erevar's grasp, and he turned her to face him.

"You see your future. I first saw this vision before any of Alecyn's deeds became clear. I saw the Waeferen's return and the True Voice's death. The first time I encountered you on Spirit Road, I recognized you for what you were. And I know why you guided Alecyn to this place. You want the Fragment, don't you?"

He hefted the object in his hand. It resembled a scroll of metal, on which chiseled inscriptions gave off a light glow. Some runes broke off unevenly when they reached the end.

Eevee stared at it blankly. Her mind was shocked by what she had seen. She was shocked further by the unmistakable ring of truth the vision had carried. She still couldn't remember anything clearly before arriving in Jonrah, but she knew what she was now.

"What... what Fragment. It keeps being referred to. I don't know what it is?"

"The Waeferen transcribed the Great Song. It made them masters of this world. But it broke when they fled. And they scattered the pieces. This is one. And you were to get it for your puppet."

"I didn't even know about it. I can't remember it."

"It imprinted on your Song, an imperative you may not even have been aware of. But in all the visions I have seen, she has the Fragments. That is why I came here tonight: to see if it was my Fragment that she gained first. Then I would know how close my death is."

Eevee struggled to free herself, but Erevar's handheld her as firmly as his power did. She couldn't imagine herself out of the woods, away from his house. His own will held her firmly. He held her up to eye level.

"I saw it tonight, traveler. It is mine. Mine is the first she gains. This must not be. Alecyn must gather the pieces together. But for me. Then, as the prophecy says, I will be the one to see her dead on the heights of Satan's Kingdom, not you."

Erevar suddenly hurled the cat from him into the deep shadows between the trees. They swallowed her, and Erevar returned to his house on the white path.

CHAPTER 7:

THE BREAKING HEART

Alecyn's mind fluttered like the pages of the book she held. She was unable to maintain her concentration on a single line of thought. Symbols, text, and musical notation flew past her eyes. Images flew through her mind. Jerad, Erevar, Rose. She had thought her stay in the Heart would be only a few days, but Erevar had been hosting them for a month as his guests, and she saw no evidence of the promised gathering of the clans. Was Erevar lying? What would he gain apart from separating her from Jerad? Why was Jerad still here? Was he waiting for her? But why? A man like that… She hummed softly as she thought about him. A new tune had suddenly appeared in her mind, but only as a fragment. She didn't know where she had heard it and could not remember more than a few bars, so she endlessly repeated them.

For the hundredth time, she shook herself mentally and tried to refocus her concentration on the task at hand. She sat cross-legged on cushions. Books and scrolls were scattered around her. A large, green book with silver pages was at the center of a web of paper. Curves and hooks covered the page in wide-spaced lines. It was a language she had never seen, but Mendel told her it was the language of the Waeferen. Something pulled her to those pages of the book written in the ancient tongue. Her Nelim assistant entered the room and took his place opposite her, the sea of books between them. He carried a pile of his own tomes and opened them to marked pages. His face was the palest blue, with darker lines creeping across his features from the ears and jawline as his expressions changed. When he was excited, his face would turn a deep royal blue.

"I found references in these works to Waeferen's musical notation, which resembles the script they use in the Prophecy. His tone emanated youthful enthusiasm, and his skin tingled darker. Erevar had sent him to help Alecyn understand the Prophecy, which told of her coming and described her prophesied actions. The young scholar eagerly jumped into the task, displaying the enthusiasm of a young puppy. He walked around with a smile and was impossible not to like, though Alecyn wished she did not feel as though it were the blind leading the blind. Or in this world, she supposed, the deaf leading the deaf.

"Do you know what they mean?" she asked, trying to dispel fatigue.

"Well, no. Not as such. But this is certainly music, not prose." He held up a stiff, silver scroll made of what appeared to be metal. "And it looks like the prophecy's first page of Waeferen's script. Don't you agree?"

Alecyn looked and hummed again before stopping herself. "Yes, it certainly looks like the same language."

"No!" gushed Mendel. "Not just the same language. Nelim and humans use unique symbols to denote music rather than words. You cannot confuse music with text. Why should the Waeferen be any different? They are of this world just like we are. Well, just like I am."

A brief flash of blue raced across his face momentarily. Embarrassment this time. "So, by comparing that text to known Waeferen music, I think we can certainly say that the Waeferen elements of the prophecy are in the form of song."

"Well, surely that must have been known before now."

"Yes, it is not all that difficult to discover. But then, the Prophecy of the True Voice has always been the domain of Erevar. I mean, that actual book. We are all familiar with the story. But Erevar has allowed no one to examine the source before now."

"Why do you think Erevar has suddenly allowed it?"

"Why, because... well, here you are. Aren't you?" Mendel had a broad smile on his face. "You should be allowed to understand the ancient text," Mendel said.

Alecyn pulled the green book closer to her, humming again. While her eyes scanned the lines of Waeferen's musical notes, she suddenly realized she had started humming a new tune. Or rather, the familiar tune that had been rolling around in her head had become longer as she had been reading. She stopped, staring at the alien markings. She began the tune again, whistling it, this time from beginning to end, and once more, her mind generated additional notes that she added to the last point she had reached.

"Alecyn…" Mendel said, watching her as she began again, singing wordlessly now. "Are you...is that….?"

"It is the Waeferen music. I have been looking at this for days, and a tune has been stuck in my head. It jumped off the page into my mind, and the more I look at it…!"

"The more it... well, jumps off the page!" Mendel laughed joyously. "I don't think even Erevar can sing Waeferen music. No one can! Weaver of lost music, Singer of lost songs." He quoted. "That is from the human lines of prophecy! Here…" He flipped the book's pages to another section of Waeferen's script. "Wait, I must try to transcribe the music you make." He experienced a sense of foolishness, blushing blue as he always did when using an unfamiliar expression. The situation started to improve, and she could perceive the music in the book, restrained only by the symbols written on the pages.

Alecyn looked at the new page and allowed her eyes to move along the lines while keeping her mind blank. A melody surfaced, and she sang it out. It was becoming easier, and she could feel the music confined to the book, chained by the symbols inscribed on the pages. She unlocked those chains now, allowing the ancient music to stretch itself in the air.

The room darkened apart from a misty light that glowed above them. Mendel's mouth gaped open, his face pale was now completely white. His nimble fingers danced across the blank pages of a book held across his lap, scribing Nelim's musical notation as Alecyn sang.

"What is this, Mendel?" Alecyn asked wonderingly. "What are we seeing?"

"It is the Waeferen music. I have read that it affected the most adept in producing images and sounds. We are seeing the Waeferen segment of the prophecy!"

The image changed. Like a bright star, a silver light appeared through the smoke and flame. It became larger, its light drowning out the burning forest. There existed a sheet of metal. No, it was a scroll-shaped sheet of metal covered in a script of curves and hooks that shone as though the fire was burning through them.

"Waeferen music," Mendel said. "That is Travelled Steel. We have lost the making of it. The Waeferen took its secret with them. Trace those notes, and the music will ring out for all to hear."

They saw a bloodied, blue hand clutching at the Travelled Steel, and then it became a human, a female hand. The flames faded, and another scroll appeared in a hand covered in a tight-fitting leather glove.

Again, it transformed into a female hand, and they pressed the two pieces together until they joined, seamlessly becoming one. Mendel gasped and began tearing through the books and scrolls the pair had strewn about them. He was mumbling and muttering in his own language. The image mesmerized Alecyn. A third piece of metallic scroll joined the first two as a black hand clenched it and dragged stone fingernails across the polished surface while pulling it out. Finally, only one piece remained in the center of the puzzle that assembled itself. She saw islands scattered against a backdrop of immense darkness through the piece. It seemed impossible for them to be so far away, but she could still observe minute details. A city of white towers, standing tall and proud against the sea. A town surrounded by a forest of stakes and moats. Its buildings are a mixture of canvas, wood, and stone. She saw Jerad walking at the head of a tide of people engaging in conversation and making hand movements. He sent men and women hurrying away to do his bidding.

Then, another city, this one a riot of color and architecture of all kinds, with no apparent plan or reason behind it. Tall cliffs rose above it, with a blazing white circle atop them. But a fog of blackness was rising like a giant wave from the sea to fall over the city. A frantic Mendel who pushed a faded, torn, leathery piece of parchment under her nose broke her attention away from the sights.

"Look, Alecyn! Look! Look! Look!" He babbled like an excited child as he traced the faded script with a shaking finger.

"One brings the Song, Hunter and Prey become One, The Fearless Song fills the Void, The Fearless Heart rekindles the Star of the East, Dawn battles Night for the Heavens Two brings the Light, three awakens the Sleeper, The Path divides..."

Alecyn looked at him blankly.

"We have seen One become Two, become Three. The One came from the hand of the Nelim, and the Two came from the hand of a human, possibly a human. The third..." He tailed off, considering what they had both seen.

"Came from a black hand. A man's hand."

"The sorcerer of Satan's Kingdom?" Mendel wondered.

"But what were they? More pieces of Waeferen music?"

"The oldest legend of the Nelim tells of the last magnificent work of the Waeferen, the act which enabled them to build the portals and escape. They transcribed part of the Great Song and became masters of... well, of everything! They can change the world to the whim of their minds. But someone broke it and lost the pieces. You recover them, to reassemble the pieces and heal this world!" His eyes shone passionately, and Alecyn recoiled from him.

"Is that how the True Voice fulfills the prophecy?"

"I believe so. Now, I believe so. And I think Erevar has one of those fragments. That is the source of his great power. It must be!"

Alecyn's mind raced. Erevar's power, his long centuries of life, his forest Heart, which kept them all safe amid an eternal paradise. Everything stemmed from his possession of one of these legendary artifacts. Part of her wished to deny it, act as if it were ridiculous, and search for practical answers. But another part of her, growing more accepting of Jonrah each day, told her it felt right. She opened her mouth to speak, and a terrifying roar shook the room.

CHAPTER 8:
THE BURNING HEART

They saw a terrible fire, a tearing inferno. Tall, dark shapes stood out against the flames, and Alecyn realized they were trees. Objects fell, trailing thick black smoke and swathed in cloying flames. Objects that withered and screamed as they fell—people and animals. With a roar, one of the dark towers leaned and then fell, with it a tangle of wooden constructs, platforms, houses, and pathways. Another tree fell as an explosion tore through its roots.

"The Heart is on fire!" Mendel whispered in horrified awe. "This cannot happen. Erevar would never allow it!"

Alecyn leaped to her feet as the room shook. Cushions and books flew. As the room tilted, Mendel's body flung from wall to wall. Alecyn had become used to thinking of the massive trees of the Heart as solid constructs. She suddenly recalled that they existed as trees. And something equally massive tilted them. A black reptilian eye suddenly appeared at one of the windows, narrowing at the sight of her. Another savage blow, and the eye was gone. But Alecyn could see their attacker flying into the distance, then turning and hurtling back towards her. It was a dragon, and fire gushed from its mouth.

"We are under attack!" Alecyn cried. "The Heart is under attack!"

"This is no vision!" Mendel shouted above the din, fighting to keep his balance. "Only the sorcerer from the Black Isle possesses the power to penetrate Erevar's defenses."

"Unless something has happened to Erevar," Alecyn said. Their eyes met for one terrified moment.

The dragon bellowed again as it swept between the trees. It burned down the trees around them. The vision was coming true. However, she suddenly realized she wasn't standing in a tree. She wasn't even standing. This place wasn't real, not physical. Which meant there was no dragon and no fire. Not if she didn't want there to be. She got to her feet and strode to the window. Her skin tightened to the point she expected it to tear and char away from her bones as the dragon pushed a wave of blistering air before it. The creature was black and covered in horns and spikes. The dragon stretched its jaws wide.

"No," Alecyn said calmly. "You are not real. I am."

The world shifted around her. The dragon slowed as though moving in slow motion. Everything had drifted. Mendel was fighting to regain his balance. Books glided through the air, pages idly fluttering.

"I don't know what you are, but I know what is real." Alecyn closed her eyes and remembered the feeling of her hand in Jerad's as they fled through the forest from the creatures of Nameless. His warm skin and reassuring grip assured her he would never let go. When they last met, the coldness in his eyes caused a feeling of betrayal. The distance that had grown between them. The heartache of wanting to hold his hand again in the real world. Those were real.

When she opened her eyes again, the dragon was gone. A woman stood in the air before her. She donned a helmet and suit of armor encased in figure-hugging metal that accentuated her female form. Alecyn knew who she faced.

"You are full of surprises, aren't you?" said the Black Hand.

Alecyn didn't answer. She looked at the fires that raged across the Heart and willed them gone. Once again, the world shifted. The fires flickered and died, returned, and then died again. The trees were whole and untouched, charred and smoking, and alight and consumed by an inferno.

"Two can play that game, sugar," the Black Hand mocked. "And I have the advantage. You still have one foot in that pathetic, tiny little world we both came from. You still deny the power of this one. I don't, which strengthens my will." She walked across the air towards Alecyn, drawing a barbed blade from her back. "It has been a long time since I had to rely on physical force to get my way. Magic is a drug. But so is blood."

She hurled the sword, end over end, towards Alecyn. Despite herself, Alecyn ducked, and suddenly the fires surrounded her. Black monstrous figures swarmed across the forest floor, undeterred by the rain of fire that fell from above. The Hand willed fire to consume the Heart, killing and maiming creatures everywhere. Alecyn fought to hold in her mind the image of the Heart as it had been, but her grip on that reality was gone. The dragon returned, bellowing in triumph as it powered through the air towards her, a serpentine neck reaching for her.

Mendel cannoned into her, wrapping his slender arms around her, and the room winked out of existence.

CHAPTER 9:
THE LOST HEART

Alecyn and Mendel stood before Erevar's house. Alecyn looked about her frantically, searching for the enemy she had been facing a moment before.

"What are you doing? I can stop her!" Alecyn shouted. In the distance, explosions shattered trees, and fires raged. Erevar's house was a ruin, but the battle had moved on. The absence of bodies was evident, but Alecyn refrained from pondering the consequences for the Nelim, who had forsaken their physical existence to dwell in this place. When the Black Hand imposed her reality of death on them, what happened to those spirits?

"She had you beat, Alecyn. Your mind isn't strong enough yet. You could beat her in a battle of magic, but her magic is not what counts. We must find Erevar!"

Alecyn wanted to will herself back into the chaos. But what Mendel said made sense. She had been no match for the Hand's will, only succeeding temporarily in destroying her illusion. She allowed Mendel to pull her along towards the house. Her Nelim attire was gone. She wore armor and mail. A sword clutched in one gauntleted fist.

"No! This isn't right. I am not a soldier. I am not a fighter!" The armor disappeared, and Alecyn was wearing the Nelim garb again.

Mendel ran ahead of her, already sifting through the timbers and stones that had once been Erevar's house.

"I feel the hold that creature has over us. I fear for Erevar. He would never allow this." Mendel gasped in pain as a smoldering beam seared his hands. "I feel her will imposing itself on everything."

Alecyn felt it, too. The destruction gained a firmer foothold. The mind of the Black Hand was taking control over more of the Heart. Mendel furiously tore at the rubble, desperate for any sign of his master, ignoring burned hands and torn flesh. Alecyn stood frozen, unable to decide. Where was Eevee? Where was Jerad? She should find them.

But without Erevar's presence, what options did she have by herself? She had already failed to match the power of the Black Hand, and the burning forest around them stood as a testament to her failure. Mendel fell back as a beam shifted beneath his feet, sending him tumbling. Tears cut runnels in the soot and grime that masked his face. It was Mendel's pain that set Alecyn's path.

If she didn't get crushed by a falling tree or roasted alive, she could wander the inferno looking for Eevee or Jerad and probably get killed by the Black Hand or one of her creatures. Or she could help someone in pain before her.

She assessed his injuries once she had pulled him out of the ruined house. His Song resonated with her, and she discovered its peculiar, alien symphony. She heard where the tune broke and sputtered into discordant noise, where it faded beyond her ability to hear. She saw the connection to the injuries his body carried and realized suddenly that he was bleeding profusely from a gash on his side.

"This must have happened when she attacked us. Mendel, why didn't you let me know you were wounded? You have broken this wound open twice as much with your climbing about, you fool!"

"My life doesn't matter. Erevar is dead or dying."

"Then he is gone and cannot help us. But I can help you. I can save you, at least."

Mendel clutched her. "This is the second life; his spirit is in all things here. We can restore him."

Alecyn looked down at Mendel sadly. "I can't. I can't bring someone back from the dead."

Mendel shook his head frantically. "His spirit is all around us, fading away. Together, we can restore this one corner of the Heart. Bring him back just for…" He stopped talking as Alecyn put a hand over his mouth.

"Stop talking! I'm not losing you, Mendel."

She focused on a tune she knew well, repeating it in her mind, closing her eyes to the destruction of the Heart. Her mind focused on the tune to the exclusion of all else. The music that was the life force of all those in the Heart came into focus. Mendel's Song foremost, but she was aware of others, too. The Nelim Songs were alien, their rhythms and melody seeming askew to Alecyn, slightly jarring to her ears. But they were nothing compared to the chaotic noise of the dark creatures that had invaded the Heart with the Black Hand. It was painful for her, and yet...

As her mind brushed the Song of the nearest of the monstrous creatures, she thought she heard the faint echo of something familiar. She dismissed it, her medical training returning her focus to the task at hand.

Mendel's wound resisted her attempts to heal it, to restore its broken passages and make it whole again. She was aware of needing more power and reached the nearest source. It came from her. A warmth suffused her. She could feel it. She heard it in the strength of her own Song, a tune so familiar that she realized it must always be on the edge of her consciousness. She drew on that power, feeling the warmth dim, and the Song faded slightly. It was enough. Mendel's Song rang out, clear and true.

The Nelim sat up, gasping for air. Alecyn fought the urge to lie down and sleep. There was a price for magic. She returned to the tune that she used to focus on. It was a simple melody, one of the first things she had learned to play. It reminded her of home. She drew on more power and searched for Erevar's Song. The painful noise of the Black Hand and her creatures became louder and closer. Alecyn's magic was drawing her. Alecyn heard snatches of Erevar's Song. But Erevar's Song was scattering and rapidly fading in snatches.

She sang, directing her power to draw those fragments together. But it was like trying to grab smoke.

"This shall not be. This shall not be."

She noticed Mendel's chanting and opened her eyes, saw the Nelim on his knees, eyes tight shut, face screwed up in concentration. And the ghostly image of Erevar's house, as she had known it, flickered into being over the ruins of what it was now. Mendel's face was deathly white; sweat covered it, and blood leaked from his nose. A faint trembling began in his shoulders and arms. She realized he was pitching every ounce of willpower into holding that image in his mind.

"Hold on, Mendel!" she muttered as she closed her eyes. The world of music was there before her, and now Erevar's Song was becoming whole.

Alecyn gave everything she had, holding nothing back. She could feel the warmth dash from her body. She Sang, and her Song shook the world. Erevar's theme came to life before her as though her Singing were holding it aloft above the cacophony of the dying Heart. When Alecyn opened her eyes, Erevar's house stood, and Erevar stood on the porch, a piece of Travelled Steel in his hands.

Mendel was on his hands and knees, groaning as he tried to keep this reality foremost. Frost covered Alecyn's skin. She couldn't feel her hands or feet. Her vision dimmed, and the color was bleeding away. Erevar walked towards them, his face a mask of sadness.

"I foresaw this moment, Alecyn. When the Heart is broken, we lose everything. My people would forever be lost. But we must survive. You and me. Or all the world will suffer the same fate as the Nelim. Come with me." He held out his hand to Alecyn.

"W-w-where?" Alecyn spoke between chattering lips.

"Away from here. This needs to be taken far from the Black Hand." He gestured with the silver scroll he held.

"I need to find Eevee," Alecyn replied, stumbling, trying to get to her feet. "And... J-J-Jerad."

Erevar shook his head sadly, casting his eyes down. "I am so sorry, Alecyn, but they are gone. We must not delay, or we will lose everything. Come, now. There is no more time."

Mendel collapsed to the ground with a groan, and Erevar's house faded back into smoldering rubble. Erevar remained, though, his spirit restored by Mendel's willpower and Alecyn's magic. Alecyn crawled to Mendel's still form. "He is... alive. Help him. P-p-please!"

A shadow flew over them from high above. It was the dragon sweeping overhead. It circled above them as though searching.

Rose had not yet located the magic she had felt, and she searched still. Erevar looked up, alarm painting his features. Dark blue flowed across his face in rapid swirls.

"We have no more time. She will sense us in a matter of moments. Come with me now!"

"I won't leave him!" Alecyn shot back. Erevar moved towards her, reaching for her, and Alecyn scrambled back on her hands.

"He does not matter! You and I do! Only we can stop the Silence and restore this world! Nothing else matters!" Erevar was snarling now. Fire exploded behind him, flinging him to the ground. The Waeferen artifact he carried slid out of his grasp, coming to rest midway between Alecyn and himself. Above, the dragon shrieked its hate and triumph as it powered down through the air towards them. With an effort that almost made her pass out, Alecyn lunged for and grabbed the scroll. Erevar's hand closed on the other side at the same time. He bared his teeth. Hate painted his features.

"It is mine!"

Alecyn clung to the silver scroll to the exclusion of all else. Its tune Sang to her, called to her. She had no strength left, no power to put into song. Her body was ice cold, and her limbs weak. Death descended on her from above, and her friends would die here in pain and fear. They had lost everything. But the tune was familiar. The tune was one she knew. It was the first tune she had ever learned to play. Her mother taught her when her grandfather gave her his flute. The Waeferen inscription lit up, and Alecyn could feel a new strength entering her body. The music inscribed on this scroll was the tune she had learned as a child!

The scroll suddenly blazed with light and heat, blasting Erevar away from it as he screamed. The dragon screamed as the wall of light hurled it away.

"No!" Erevar howled. "It is mine! You were to be my weapon against the Silence. I have seen it. I have set the path! This cannot be!"

Alecyn was one with the Song of the Scroll. It was a perfect counterpoint to her own Song, merging with it, separate yet united. Together, they formed a glorious symphony, and Alecyn had never felt such power.

Once more, she reached for Mendel, lifting his flagging life force. She took his hand as she got to her feet, pulling him with her. "I will not dance to your tune, Erevar. I will find my friends, and then I will help the people of the Southlands. I don't care about your plans!"

"Your friends are dead, you foolish child! I killed Eevee myself!" Erevar spat. "And your barbarian human friend…" He didn't get to finish.

"You did what?!" Alecyn shouted. But her shout rang through the air, drowning out the falling trees and the raging fires. Erevar shrank away from it. The Waeferen scroll was now incandescent in Alecyn's hands.

"She would have destroyed you. She was one of them! And when you reached your potential, she would have killed you. I did it to secure our future!"

Anger boiled in Alecyn now. She forgot her lessons. Forgot her medical training. She forgot herself. The boiling rage growing in her since she had found herself in this world wiping everything clean.

They had taken her from her home. They had destroyed her life and flung her into a battle she had not chosen and did not want. And now, this creature had murdered her only friend so that he could continue to pull the strings on Alecyn's life. Power filled her, but it wasn't enough. There was power all around her, and she drew on it. It came from Erevar, Rose, every Nelim and twisted creature, and the dying fabric of the Heart itself. She was a god.

She could feel Jerad distantly. He fought back-to-back with a Nelim warrior surrounded by black armored creatures that were a mixture of insects and humans. Scores of dead Nelim and monsters lay in a circle around them. She searched for Eevee but could find no trace of her. Grief washed over her and fueled her infinite anger. She became aware of Erevar running away from her and laughed at the futility of the gesture. She could feel Rose standing and watching. The woman was suddenly wary and ready to return to the real world in a heartbeat.

Alecyn struck out with all the force she could muster. It was a scream, and it was directed at Erevar. His spirit was torn asunder. The noise of Alecyn's assault masked his own scream. Rose fled before Alecyn could turn her rage on her. Alecyn's anger flowed out of her like water from a burst dam. The grief remained. And something else. Her compassion. She sang, and her song gathered all of those she could still sense. Jerad, Mendel, and Nelim of both high and low-born. She drew them to her and stepped out of the burning Heart and back into Jonrah. There existed a sense of transition. The feeling of traveling was apparent. Some of those spirits forcefully wrenched away. She understood they were the ones, like Erevar, who had no existence beyond the Heart. Her tears followed their path as she felt them slipping through her fingers. She couldn't save them.

CHAPTER 10:
SILENCE FALLS

Rose awoke with her face pressed to a cold stone. Her body had nothing but a fine sheen of sweat. Where her skin had lain against the frigid floor for too long, it felt numb. She tried to move and almost wept from the pain in muscles that had not moved for hours. Her head throbbed, and as she tried to lift it, she sank beneath a wave of nausea. Shifting onto her side, she vomited, her stomach heaving until there was nothing left. She lay in the center of a circular room of plain stone. One curving wall displayed deeply incised runic shapes, interspersed with words and letters that humans recognized, though in various languages.

An arcade facing the wall looked out over a steep-sided valley. Broken slabs of rock comprised the far side. This represented the tallest of the Tall Towers of Nameless. Here, her body had rested in a meditative trance while her mind waged war in the spirit realm of the Heart.

"Mistress?" came a tentative inquiry. Rose looked up with bloodshot eyes. One of her acolytes had entered the room and now knelt beside her, robes draped across his arms to cover her. He must have entered the room to check on her, strictly against her orders. Fury, comforting and familiar, boiled within her. That a slave should see her so reduced! Her will was a black ocean, carefully damned but ready to be unleashed. She slapped a hand against the stone floor, lashing out with her mind to direct the Noise against the intruder. The impact should have turned his bones to jelly. But she was weak. Instead, the force of her attack flung him across the room like a gale, causing him to slam against the wall. His head bounced, and he slid into an unconscious but living heap.

She forced herself to her feet and pulled the dark robes about herself. Casually walking barefoot across the room, she sang a soft, seductive aria, weaving her fingers in a complex dance as she did. As she passed the servant, her fingers stiffened as though flinging something from their tips. A black net flew from her fingers to envelop the unfortunate man. His eyes fluttered open as they tightened, smoke curling from his flesh wherever the dark strands touched him. As Rose pulled open the door to her inner sanctum, she paused, eyes closed to drink in the sounds of agonized death. She took strength from them.

Beyond the sanctum, a chamber draped with silks and dominated by a large, canopied bed. A dozen men and women awaited her there. All of them, if dressed at all, wore scanty clothing, and had the same perfect physique. Some rushed to her side with expressions of utter devotion, their minds empty except for the adoration she had put there. Others cowered in fear. Both emotions pleased her, and usually, she would have taken her time choosing between the willing and unwilling slaves at her command. But not now.

She screamed, a howl of frustrated rage. All her plans lay in ruins! She did not see the swirling vortex that opened in the center of the room and into which her scream poured. She was blind to the fate of her beautiful playthings, who found themselves pulled into that vortex, limbs snapping as they tried to cling to furniture or each other. The Black Hand wished to be alone, and she did not care for the fate of slaves.

She had been so close. The Nelim traitor had given her the secret to entering the Heart. She had ripped the skin of Erevar's fortress and burnt it down from the inside. But it wasn't the invasion that some dreamed of, like the foolish Atramen. Not armies and battles. She alone had invaded the Heart. Her body had not moved from the inner sanctum, but her mind had walked through the sylvan idylls of the Heart. And she had changed it to suit her. The invasion took Erevar by surprise. She had ridden the consciousness of one of the Nelim until she was close enough to strike at Erevar himself. With his mind neutralized, there had been none within the Heart with a will strong enough to oppose her.

But she had not been able to find the Fragment. And then Alecyn had interfered, and Rose had found herself expelled from the dreamscape of the Heart by a force the likes of which she had only experienced in the presence of Kragen Onyx. She had a feeling of being cold. She had spent so much of her life living in fear of her father, of being alone. This world had been her escape from that. Onyx had given her power, which her old life never gave her. In Jonrah, she did not experience fear until now.

She sat on the bed, staring into space. Onyx would soon require her report. He would expect to hear that Erevar was dead, the vaunted Nelim dream fortress destroyed, and that the Black Hand possessed a Fragment of the Great Song. She knew this final thing was the only thing he cared about. She remembered the fury when he discovered Atramen's betrayal. The coward used the Fragment he had taken from Argent to seal himself and his city behind the Veil and out of Onyx's reach. That his acolyte should now possess the potential for greater power than his master. She berated herself for her inactivity. There must be a way around this. She still controlled Nameless and its legions. She needed to discover where Alecyn had materialized when her spirit left the Heart. There had to be a way!

A bell rang, and Rose stood, looking about the room frantically. "No! Not yet..." her voice tailed off before the dull, graveyard tolling of the bell. As its mournful lament echoed around her, a flickering, cold blue light filled the room. The walls dissolved, stone peeling away. As the walls peeled away, a new scene became visible. Darkness, lit by a flickering, staccato flare. She saw tall figures hunched and vaguely human except for their heads in that flashing, stuttering illumination.

The creatures had the heads of ravens. They wore black robes from which skeletal human arms emerged, and shining black eyes stared unblinking above steel-tipped beaks. They flanked a dais, atop which was a chair and, in the chair...

Rose prostrated herself on the floor, her breath coming in gasps. There existed a void in that chair, that throne. A black man-shape whose outline flickered and distorted as though in constant flux. He had shown her his face in all her previous meetings with him. Or, at least, he had shown her a face. Whichever he chose for the occasion. That he appeared to her cloaked was a sign of his displeasure. As the throne room solidified around her, she realized his court's cackling, growling, braying cacophony. The Ravenguards were not the only macabre beings that swore allegiance to the black sorcerer. The War of the Song had produced atrocities of nature, which Onyx had gathered about himself.

"The Black Hand returns." came a sonorous, smooth voice. "What news, daughter?"

"The Heart is destroyed. Erevar is dead."

There was silence. Onyx waited.

"I... I could not locate the Fragment." Rose began. "But I know where it is."

"And who has it now? I can take it from her…"

The noise from the bestial court around her rose to a painful screech. She covered her ears, feeling blood trickling from them. The creatures gathered closer, enjoying her pain.

"The human has it? Yes, she must. Erevar must have given it to her. The Prophecy…"

"Do not tell me of the Prophecy, human. I authored most of it."

"I saw it. I saw the Fragment. She was singing it!"

Silence. The court stilled. The shape on the throne rose and then became a black whirlwind, howling towards her. It engulfed her, picking her up off the ground and holding her aloft. A face loomed close to hers from the swirling blackness filling her vision.

"It allowed her to use it?" The voice was soft once more, carrying a menace that chilled Rose. For an instant, the memory of her father flashed in her mind - the smell of booze on his breath, the eerie silence before the violence erupted. The fear made her want to cry and cower, but even as it swept over her, she felt another emotion ignite within her. Anger.

"Yes! That makes her more powerful than you, doesn't it? Because you could never awaken your Fragment, even after all the years you have spent hiding away on your island trying! Hiding while I wield true power out in the world. Me and Atramen!"

A part of her screamed to stop. She knew that her words would result in her being ripped apart. But she let the rage flow. She lashed out, her words carrying her power and directed like knives. She stabbed at the black sorcerer, slicing at the whirling darkness. She glimpsed the court as though through a scudding storm cloud with each cutting word. Onyx's creatures screamed in pain; they cowered and flinched.

Onyx deflected her attack on them, letting them carry the pain intended for him. As he had taught her, Rose drew power from those creatures, drinking in their agony and flinging it back at her master. Words degraded into pure Noise. Her limbs thrashed as though she held knives in her hands instead of her Voice.

Suddenly, the wind was gone. Without warning, the wind vanished and flung Rose away, causing her to land in a bruised and winded heap. The court was silent. All around lay the bodies of warped creatures. A man lay at the foot of the throne, slowly picking himself up. He was bald, his face young-looking, skin smooth and hairless. He wore simple black clothes, a tunic, and trousers and walked barefoot. His dark eyes glittered with hatred across the room at her. The Ravenguard still stood, and in a word, they advanced. Their black robes flung wide, revealing wings resembling bats. Their emaciated torsos split along a line down their middle to reveal a gaping aperture lined with needle teeth.

Arching their necks, they let out their hunting shouts and propelled themselves into the air. Rose could do nothing. To attack Onyx had taken all her strength. And it hadn't been enough. She was utterly drained.

She closed her eyes and waited for her bloody death. A shouted command rang across the room, leaving a curious ringing. She opened her eyes and saw the Ravenguard around her, the closest inches away, poised to strike. Every one of them were froze in place. Onyx walked towards her, stepping around the statue-like figures of his bodyguard. They were still. Held by his order. It seemed as if time had frozen them in place.

"I did not realize you had become so strong, Rose," Onyx said softly. "It has been too long since you were here. I see I have repeated my mistake with Atramen, haven't I? Mmm?"

"No, master." Rose breathed. "I am still yours always." He had to believe that. She wouldn't die here!

"Then why do you fight me?"

"Because I do not want to die. I am no use to you dead. But you would kill me out of anger with no thought to the future."

"No, I wouldn't. I would not waste such a useful commodity. But I would have hurt you a great deal." He looked at her with his head tilted as though examining a new species. "You witnessed this other human use the Fragment?"

"Yes. She used it to escape the Heart and took all the survivors with her."

"How many survivors?"

"There were few. Thirty maybe. Warriors."

"And you can track them?"

"My creatures can track them."

"My creatures, Rose. My creatures. I allow you to command them, but they are mine. Mine." Onyx gently reprimanded her.

"Of course." Rose bowed her head in acquiescence.

"You will pursue and recover the Fragment. And if along the way you come across Atramen. Be sure to kill him, too."

"Yes, lord." Onyx turned away from her, and she allowed herself to breathe.

"This setback requires a change in strategy, though. And I am not pleased at having to do that." He turned back to her, watching her with fathomless eyes. "Humans cannot possess two pieces of the Song. That was one thing Atramen did for us, taking it out of the hands of the Higher Hundred. But they still have one. And if they ally with this woman, they will have two again."

"I will take Atramen's Fragment from his dead hands," Rose growled.

"No, you won't. I no longer trust you as I once did. I am sending one of my pets to watch over you. He will take possession of the Fragments. And feast on your eyes if you try to lay a finger on one of them yourself."

With a mumbled, growling litany, one of the Ravenguards came to life. It settled itself to the ground behind Rose, clawed hands resting on her shoulders. Onyx sang, and the pressure of its hands was gone. The monstrous guard was gone, with an ordinary raven in its place. It flew up into the air to settle on her shoulder, its yellow eyes never leaving its master. Rose noted that its beak was still steel-tipped, and its claws seemed too overlarge.

"What use is this to me? Atramen has Mutes and Shriekers by the thousands!" Rose protested.

"It is of use to me," replied Onyx, taking his place on the throne again. "When the time comes, he will resume his accustomed form and then…" He smiled faintly. "You know why I chose these creatures as my bodyguard."

"And what will you do while we recover your fragment?"

"I shall deprive the wizards in Welcome of what they think is safely guarded. Who will betray his colleagues, city, and world?"

CHAPTER II:

INTO THE SOUTHLANDS

Sunlight pecked at her eyelids. A terrible exhaustion held her in its grip, and it took an effort to open her eyes. She squinted at the bright daylight falling through chinks in an interlaced canopy of trees. Alecyn had no knowledge of the soreness in her muscles until she tried to sit up. Pain shrieked through her limbs, her back, and her stomach. A groan escaped her lips, and a face came into view. Pale blue skin, now flushed with flowing patterns of royal blue and concerning eyes.

"Alecyn. Don't move too much. Your body will be very weak and quite sore."

"Mendel... what... where... what happened?" Alecyn whispered. Her throat was raw, and her mouth dry. He passed a water skin between her lips, encouraging her to sip.

"I do not know where we are, but the warriors are scouting our position. We can only hope we are far from Nameless."

"We're...we are not...in the Heart?" She tried to sit up, but Mendel pushed her down gently.

"Let your body recover its strength. You used great energy to bring so many of us out of the Heart before it…" Mendel broke off and looked away. Distress painted his face. "You drew power from all around you. I have never seen such magic firsthand, but I understand it always comes with great pain."

Alecyn gave up the struggle to lift her head and gazed at the trees. The surrounding woods did not differ from the Heart, but she fancied that she felt the difference.

Something dug uncomfortably into her backside, and she reached underneath. Her flute was in her back pocket. She wore jeans, sneakers, and a sweater again, too. She held the flute in front of her. In the Heart, she had been so focused on other things she had not thought about manifesting the instrument. But now that she was back in the physical world, she felt like she had reunited with an old friend. She put it to her lips and blew a short ditty, a dancing melody, half improvised. The sound brought back memories of home, as it always did. Her aches seemed to subside slightly, her head clearing. Mendel sat back, with one hand resting on her shoulder. He closed his eyes as she played, enjoying the music. Alecyn didn't feel the need to focus consciously on his Song, the music of the surrounding land, or that of those she had brought out of the Heart. It was all there, and her awareness took it in instinctively. She was learning.

"Alecyn!" a male voice called. She recognized Jerad's voice and lifted herself into a sitting position before she had time to think of it. Her muscles screamed their protests anew. She was in a forest dell, sunlight slanting through gaps in the trees above and falling across a floor of tall grass and wildflowers. Ancient logs, swathed in moss and half mulched, gave the floor of the Dell an uneven appearance. Somewhere, the water babbled. It was idyllic, and for a second, she wondered if they had really escaped the Heart.

But this is real—the feel of damp grass, the earthy smell of rotting wood and rich soil. The itch of long-bladed grass tickled her skin. Jerad hurried to her from across the Dell, hurdling logs and arriving on his knees beside her.

"You are awake. Are you... well?" His face was flushed, and Alecyn felt her own cheeks growing hot. A group of Nelim warriors that had broken away from the others watched with curiosity. Alecyn smiled.

"I think so. I'm not sure I am altogether here yet. Wherever here is."

She wanted to take his hand, and he raised his own as though reaching for her. But then he put them down, planting them on the ground firmly.

"We are in the Southlands. Vanja is leading a scouting party to find out exactly where. These trees are frost oaks. They grow in the deep woods between Fearnot and Ghoul's Creek."

With Mendel's help, Alecyn levered herself into a more comfortable sitting position.

"I brought us here, didn't I?"

"According to your friend, yes."

"The Black Hand was inside the Heart. She destroyed it."

Jerad nodded. "We fought, but it was hopeless... like a dream... every movement too slow, every blow just ineffectual. We were being slaughtered."

"You were not fighting real enemies. It was all about her. She imagined a Heart in which her creatures were an unstoppable army, running wild...." A thought suddenly occurred to Alecyn, and she looked at Mendel. "Erevar! I... we..."

Mendel shook his head sadly. "Erevar is no more. You..." He swallowed. "You destroyed him."

Jerad stared at her, unbelieving.

"The Black Hand had already undone him. I conjured his spirit back into existence, but... I do not believe the being who returned to us was truly Erevar." Mendel said. "Something had been lost. Some quality had disappeared."

"No, Mendel. We saw his true nature. I am sorry. He killed Eevee, and I couldn't stop him. He wanted to use me, pulling my strings like I was nothing." A terrible, raw grief rose in her. Grief for her lost friend, her best friend. Grief for the act she had committed. There was no explaining or rationality. She had killed. Tears coursed down her cheeks.

"Eevee..." she whispered brokenly. "Eevee."

Mendel crouched beside her, frozen with indecision as she wept. Jerad put his arms around her shoulders and pulled her to him. Alecyn sobbed into his chest.

****

A cookfire crackled and spat, wafting through the trees with the smell of wood, smoke, and roasting food. The Nelim gathered around it, their bodies silhouetted against the firelight in angular, hunched shapes.

An assortment of stones and other forest debris marked out a makeshift map on the ground. Jerad and Alecyn sat in front of it, and the Nelim ringed around them. Mendel refused to allow the warriors to push him aside and maintained his place by Alecyn's side. The largest of them, whom Jerad had introduced as Vanja, squatted beside Jerad.

Vanja's patrol had returned in the early evening and sketched out the terrain they had found themselves in. Jerad had estimated where they were in relation to Fearnot, and talk had turned to military strategy. Alecyn had told herself it was important to pay attention to and understand as much of the situation as possible. But the thought of planning a battle, planning to fight and kill, awoke a bitter anger in her. She sat quietly and thought of Eevee.

She experienced a sense of being disconnected. Eevee differed from how she had been at home, but the changes in her had just made Alecyn feel even closer to her. Now she could talk to her. She felt lost without Eevee's acerbic common sense, sharp comments, and barking remarks. Jerad leaned over the map, marking landscape features, pointing with a stick. She looked at his profile in the firelight. He was handsome and made her feel safe. Even here, where she knew there was a hostile army of nightmares and a psychotic sorceress hunting for her. Back home, there had been a few guys for whom she had believed she might develop feelings. But none had lasted.

Something had always held her back, causing her to back away as the relationship seemed to grow deeper. She had told herself it was because she wanted to wait for marriage before she slept with a man, that they wouldn't understand the old-fashioned notion, and that she did not have the time. Her career and voluntary work were important to her and not something she had been prepared to put aside to make time for a man.

She wondered at those thoughts now as she watched Jerad. She realized no man since her dad had ever made her feel safe.

But he did. She wondered what marriage in the world of Jonrah even looked like. Stop it, silly girl! She could almost hear Eevee in her mind. Do you want to stay here for the rest of your life? Was that ever the plan? It wasn't. It could never be. She hugged her knees to her chest, caressing the Irish flute. This wasn't her home.

She would help these people as best she could, but finding a way home had to be her priority. The thought didn't comfort her as it once would have.

"Can the female help?"

Suddenly, Alecyn realized all eyes were on her. Vanja had spoken, but to her embarrassment, she did not know what they had been discussing.

Mendel stepped in smoothly.

"Alecyn." He put emphasis on her name. Despite being unable to meet Vanja's stare, he bravely insisted on showing respect. "Has used great strength in bringing so many of us out of the Heart, and it will take time to recover from such an effort."

"Alecyn, to reach Fearnot, we must leave behind the central highlands, where we are now, amongst the frost oaks." Jerad pointed to a point on the makeshift map. "And then we will be amongst the lowlands, which will be rife with Atramen's forces."

"We saw campfires in the distance. On the horizon." In a tone of impatience Vanja added. He had already explained this. "They covered an extensive area. A sizeable force spread out." He extended a hind limb to sweep an area between a moss-covered stone that denoted their position and another representing Fearnot.

"If we go down into the lowlands, we must fight." Jerad continued. "The more we fight, the more attention we bring to ourselves. Shriekers can communicate with each other over long distances. Encounter one, and all will know exactly where we are."

"So, you want me to transport all of us to Fearnot using magic?"

"You have done it before."

"But Jerad, that was just me and Eevee. One girl and one cat. And bringing all of us here took more than I had."

"It doesn't need to be done now. We can travel to the highlands for a week. But then..." Jerad trailed off.

Alecyn considered conscious of the sharp Nelim eyes on her. She suppressed a desire to agree to impress Jerad. She had nothing to prove to him!

"I will try." She said finally. "But I am not promising anything. I am not sure I can do what I did before."

Jerad squeezed her shoulder and winked. Alecyn turned away and berated herself as she felt butterflies in her stomach. The Nelim's voices rose excitedly, discussing how to use her power best to surprise their enemy. She turned back determinedly. She would not let these warmongers use her as a weapon.

"Stop!" Her voice rang out sharply and cut through the rising babble. "None of you understand the power or what it means to wield it. None of you have the first clue about magic. And I am still learning. Mendel and I will study how to use the power. I must get us all safely to Fearnot. And I will explain to you how to use it. Is everyone clear?"

She looked around with a challenging stare. "I am not a weapon!" Several Nelim flinched visibly as though slapped. Some pulled back slightly from where she sat. She realized that without consciously thinking of it, she had drawn power from within herself and pushed it into her words. All around the fire, they were reminded of the true power hidden within the quiet human female.

A ripple of assent and bowed heads went through the gathered warriors.

She heard two themes rising in anthems of blaring pride: one from Mendel and the other from Jerad.

"Good. Now, I need to sleep." She said as she rose and walked away from the firelight to the sheltered spot that Mendel had chosen for them. Mendel followed her. He squeezed her shoulder as they walked. She looked at him in time to catch a wide grin splitting his face. She could not help but smile in return. She was done with letting others choose her path for her. She didn't look back nor see Jerad looking after her as she walked away.

The night cooled away from the fire, and Alecyn tried to burrow into the bed of ferns and soft undergrowth that Mendel had used to make a bed for her. He sat next to her, and they huddled together for warmth. He cast his cloak about them. All the Nelim had when they emerged from the Heart were their clothes and one or two pieces of weaponry or most familiar possessions. Just as Alecyn had subconsciously formed an image of herself in earth clothes, with her flute and phone, the Nelim warriors had emerged armored and armed, each with their most favored weapon. In Mendel's case, he carried a bulky backpack that Alecyn suspected contained books. She rested her head on his shoulder, enjoying the faint, slightly tangy scent that all the Nelim seemed to have. Mendel was the closest thing she had now to a friend.

"Alecyn…" Mendel began slowly. "I can see a way to do what Vanja asks."

"How?" Alecyn asked.

"I did not want to reveal this to the others." He continued, lowering his voice. "Nor did I want to raise it until you could... that is when you were…"

"It's ok, Mendel. I know what you're getting at. What is it?"

Mendel had taken something out of his backpack and passed it to her under the cloak. She could feel the cold, hard-edged metal. As she moved her hand along its sleek surface, she could feel the engravings etched into it, and in an instant, her memory came rushing back.

"It is the Waeferen Song Fragment that you took from Erevar," Mendel whispered, his eyes never leaving the group around the fire. "You Sang it in the Heart. You sang the music of the Waeferen, which no one has done since they left this world. Not even Erevar!"

Alecyn pushed the fragment away from her.

"Keep this hidden, Mendel. I don't want to see it."

He took it from her wordlessly. "We should study it in the time we have. If you can unlock even a tenth of its power…"

"No!" Alecyn hissed. "Take it out of my sight. I mean it, Mendel."

He met her eyes and nodded, wordlessly taking the fragment, and putting it back into his backpack.

"I don't even know how it came here with us. I certainly didn't conjure it out of the Heart." Alecyn said.

"Nor I. If it is here, it is because it was here. I will not mention it again, but no artifact of Waeferen's craft is ever simply an object. It may not allow us to ignore it."

Alecyn closed her eyes wearily. "It's a worry for tomorrow, Mendel."

CHAPTER 12:
FEARNOT

Lucas flexed his fingers on the reins. Frost coated the padded leather gauntlets he wore. Despite the thick wool inside the gloves, his hands were in constant danger of going numb if he kept them still for too long. He looked over his shoulder at the rest of his flight. Six stormbirds were aligned to his mount, Cullhain. Three were present on each side. They flew in a V formation, each bird heavily laden with boulders gathered from the Hasten Mountains. Like Lucas, each rider wore thick leather and wool. Goggles masked their faces, a rare commodity with lenses made from transparent other stone garnered long ago from portals. They wrapped scarves around the lower half of their faces while wearing leather helmets that covered their heads. Lucas' flyers included both men and women, all frozen solid in layers of frost.

He made a thumbs-up sign and waited to see it returned from Davin, Indra, and Jan. Then he looked over the opposite shoulder. Harken didn't return the signal. His bird drifted slightly out of formation. He was a weak link. He knew how to fly, but he was older by ten years than any other flyer and seemed vulnerable to the cold. Kraken, his stormbird, fell away from the others. It was an instinct. Stormbirds were not social animals by nature.

Lucas cursed himself for not grounding Harken. They weren't far from their target. The sick had no place in a raid. He desperately willed Harken to bring himself out of it, to lift his head, give the signal, and pull back into formation. He considered aborting the raid. But he couldn't.

Their aim was an enemy convoy transporting a war horn. He had seen the massive weapons installed on the walls of Atramen's palace in Argent. Scouting flights had revealed the horns being transported around the far eastern edge of the Hasten mountains and along roads constructed ahead of them. Based on the prisoner's account, one of those weapons could quickly demolish the hastily constructed walls surrounding Fearnot. So far, Lucas and the other Stormriders had prevented any from being brought to bear.

Finally, Harken responded. He gave the thumbs up. Lucas repeated the gesture, nodding emphatically. Harken answered back and started making corrections to his flight. Lucas hoped he was up to it. He returned to scanning the horizon. They flew above the clouds to avoid detection, which made it difficult to establish when they were coming within range of their target. If they dropped too soon, someone would spot them. The enemy had suffered enough losses to stormbird attacks that they always had sky watchers now.

He had drawn a map with charcoal onto a piece of paper. It remained firmly attached to the inside wrist of his gauntlet. He scrutinized it, noting the position of hills and mountains compared to the 'x,' which marked the expected position of the horn. It was time. He checked back over his shoulders again and was pleased to see the other riders also checking their maps, leaning out of the saddle to peer through the clouds before giving the thumbs up again to confirm. He gave the signal to begin their descent. Then, using heels against the bird's neck and hands on the reins, he urged Cullhain down. Behind him, the rest of the flight lined up on their leader, descending through the clouds in a single file. They passed through the clouds. Cullhain's long, thin tongue whipped from his beak to lap the moisture. Then, the world opened below them.

Quilted forests adorned the landscape. Flat and silent. Smoke curled lazily skyward in a dozen thin columns in the middle distance. Those were the fires of the laborers who cut down the trees and leveled the ground for the war horns to follow. With his skilled eye, he carefully traced his way through the forested land, searching for the line of the road and the stone object it had been constructed for. The camp would be just ahead of the furthest construction, and the horn would be not far behind. There! Cullhain aligned perfectly with it. He made slight adjustments, bringing the birds around so that they followed the road. The bombardment would be easier with the length of the road to sight along. He was unable to hear anything yet. There would be Mutes down there with the horn, though.

Cullhain dropped vertically now, forcing Lucas to grip the bird's neck with his thighs until his muscles screamed in protest. He saw the Mutes looking up and opening their faceplates. Cullhain shrieked in defiance and defense, attempting to drown out the Noise directed up at him by the Mutes. Lucas was almost deaf from the layers of padding he wore. As the Noise from the Mutes hit them, Lucas realized a growing buzz, a ringing in his ears, and tried to ignore it. Cullhain tossed his head, clearly aware of the same irritation.

Close now. Projectiles filled the air. Cullhain's feathers served as armor, but Lucas prayed the projectiles would not hit his vulnerable eyes. Or himself, for that matter! He pulled on a tether, gathering the tension, ready to open the huge sacks Cullhain carried. Now! He yanked the tether, letting the enormous boulders fall. Then he pulled hard on the reins, and Cullhain pulled out of his dive. As they soared skyward again, he looked back over his shoulder.

The other stormbirds followed his attack, their rocks slamming into the horn quickly. Lucas whooped behind his mask as he saw part of the horn's bell-shaped mouth disintegrate in a shower of shards and stone dust. Holes appeared elsewhere as chunks of granite the size of a man hurtled through. He banked Cullhain, circling him high enough to avoid either arrows or noise. Five birds rose unscathed from their attack runs. Harken was the sixth. Lucas saw that he had mistimed pulling out of his dive. He was too low. Kraken's impact with the war horn obliterated the remnants. One of his wings crumpled as bones shattered from the impact. Mutes leaped from all sides, hurling themselves high enough to land on the stricken bird.

Harken tried to unbuckle himself, reaching for the blade strapped to his back. As Lucas watched helplessly, a Mute came up behind him and, with one savage movement, tore out his throat. Blood geysered skyward. Harken fell back limply, sliding off Kraken's back to the ground. Lucas' first instinct was to take Cullhain back into the fight and tear into the Mutes swarming over Kraken. But a cold, inhuman voice in his mind told him that the stormbirds were only an advantage if they were airborne. On the ground, the Mutes had superiority. The rest of the flight circled, looking at him for their orders. They wanted to go back down.

Lucas made a quick slashing gesture with his thumb across his throat. This was the signal to abort. If they attacked for revenge or to recover Harken's body, not all of them would return. They could not afford to lose either stormbirds or riders.

He signaled to return home and guided Cullhain into the lead position. He didn't look back, and he hated himself for it.

****

They topped the high moorlands which bordered Fearnot to the north and came within sight of the city. For the city, it now was. Fearnot had swelled to ten times its previous size as people from the surrounding countryside had flocked to the relative safety of its walls. When news reached them that Ghoul's Creek had been taken, those numbers became a flood.

Every farmstead from the west coast to the east had emptied into Fearnot, and now the town of Ghoul's Creek, too. Or the survivors, at least. Tents stretched south over what had been the old ditch and palisade. Fearnot no longer had the river Tar marking its eastern boundary. They built a stone wall to mark the swollen community's new farthest point. It was a ramshackle affair, comprising stones from the fells and mountains brought by Stormbirds. The stormbirds left the boulders where they dropped and filled the gaps between the uneven stones with mortar. Some of the stones used were like cliff faces towering over the city.

The attacks on those walls came regularly. Mutes first, then humans in their masses. It confused him at first. The Mutes were so superior to the infantry. Why use human troops at all? The answer had come to him. Atramen did not have an unlimited supply of Mutes. Lucas knew where they came from. He knew that converting humans into Mutes must take a long time. Otherwise,

Fearnot's enemies would have overrun it long ago. It gave him hope they could hold out until Jerad returned with the True Voice.

The stormbirds came to the ground atop the Aviary, the nickname given to the hilltop where the stormbirds had built a temporary root. Lucas wearily climbed off the back of Cullhain and walked away, pulling off gloves and helmet as he did so. Blake Halmen was there as usual, marshaling a crowd of boys who helped care for the stormbirds, feeding and grooming them. Lucas saw him counting the stormbirds.

“We lost Kraken,” Lucas said numbly. Blake nodded, his flat features barely changing. "We won't be able to replace it for another month," Lucas said numbly.

“See if you can bring one fledgling along faster, will you?” Lucas asked. Blake nodded and, without a word, hurried off to his charges.

Adellin waited for Lucas at the edge of the landing field. She handed him a steaming tankard that smelled like hot cider. He gulped at it greedily. She also handed him a chunk of bread.

“Not good?” she asked, looking at his ashen face.

He looked at her as though wondering who she was.

“No. We lost Harken as well,” he finally replied.

Adellin held a hand to her mouth. Her Ghoul’s Creek accent was broad, stronger than Lucas’s or Harken’s. “Oh god, I hope it was quick.”

Lucas nodded. “It’s my fault.” He said, his voice was broken and despairing. “I should have grounded him. I saw he was weak. I should not have allowed him to put himself in that position. Now he is dead, and we have lost a good stormbird…” He trailed off. “God’s Noise! Listen to me. I think I care more about a bird than a human being.”

Adellin took his hand, pressing her face to his shoulder. She couldn't help but notice that blood smeared from his coat into his golden hair.

"That's not true, Lucas." She whispered.

"Yes, it is. I am thinking about it now. Thinking how long it takes to rear and train a stormbird compared to a rider. I am a monster!" His voice was hoarse now. Adellin hugged him fiercely, and he returned the embrace.

"You are not a monster, Lucas. But a general. You think the way a general thinks. You have had to. Who else is ready to lead us? Hmmm?"

"I am no Jerad Palene, that's for sure," Lucas mumbled. However, he wondered if Jerad also heard that cold, emotionless voice in the back of his head. This was the burden all leaders carried. To lead was to give up part of your humanity.

"No, you're not. You are Lucas Haverford. And it is thanks to you we are still alive."

"The stormbirds saved us from being overrun. I was there, remember? I saw how fast it happened."

"You just need rest. Come on. You need to sleep." She steered him away from the landing field towards the long, low timber building erected on one side. It was a dorm for stormbird riders. It had been Lucas' idea that riders would always be close to the field should an attack come.

Another figure hurried across the field now. Lucas stopped. Adellin shot a frustrated look up at him and then glared at the approaching man.

"Hayden, can't you see he's exhausted? It can wait."

Hayden grimaced and shrugged. "Sorry, Del, but it can't wait. Lucas, Asher has called an emergency council meeting. He's calling for a vote on using the Prisoner as a go-between with Atramen."

"He's what!" Lucas yelled. His fatigue sluiced from his body.

"He tried to get the vote through while you were away, but we have him deadlocked. Avery and Seth support him. Blake and I disagree. Earl and Tobias don't know which way to vote. Or they didn't. If Asher wants a vote, he may have decided."

"We need to put a stop to this. Adellin, find Jan and tell her I need as many storm riders as you can muster at the Hall."

"But…"

"Please, Del." He took her hands, pulling her close. "This is important. After this, I will follow any order you give."

Adellin gave a frustrated growl and whirled away. She turned back before she had taken a step and planted a kiss on Lucas' lips. He watched her go for a moment, politics and war forgotten. Hayden coughed politely, breaking the spell. Energized, Lucas began striding away.

"Asher's always been a problem on the Council," Hayden said. "Especially since Jerad left…" He trailed off.

"Jerad is coming back," Lucas told him firmly. "With the True Voice."

"Yes," Hayden replied, his tone unconvinced.

It had been Asher who had put Lucas forward for the leadership of the Council. Lucas had been the one who returned to Fearnot to warn of the coming war. He had insisted on preparations being made to defend the town. And they proved him right.

"Asher saw me as someone he could manipulate. I don't think he expected me to have ideas of my own. So, now he is trying to take control and use the prisoner. I will not let him gamble everyone's lives on an idiotic power play!"

The streets bustled with people going about their business with the harassed looks of people with too much to do and too little time. Others were more listless. They were refugees. Uprooted from their lives and trades. They had pinned all their hopes on reaching Fearnot and safety, but now they didn't know what to do. Lucas received smiles and nods as he walked. The Storm Riders were all well-known by now and hailed as heroes.

Lucas had the impression that his head was about to explode. Everywhere he looked, there was more that needed to be done. "Hayden. We need to do something about this. I need lists of what trades these people have, and we need to get them to work. If half the town is working to feed the other half, we will have a riot."

"I know. I tried to get the Council to agree to act. But Asher is determined to take over."

"Then don't go through the Council. Get the women going amongst the new folk and ask them what they can do." He was angry at the inertia he was seeing from everyone except Asher. To Lucas, the Council had always been wise, knowing what needed to be done and ensuring it happened. But now he saw how heavily they had all relied on Jerad to guide them. He wanted to shake them.

The Council chambers lay ahead, and he heard raised voices from inside. Lucas pushed open the tall double doors and strode in. The first thing he saw was the captive Shrieker. Ademar sat at one end of the hall. They had gagged him and bound his hands and feet. He still wore his blood-red robes, though they had gotten rid of the torture tools and his mask. The man looked as though he were dying. His skin a pasty white and tight over his skull. His eyes had a tinge of yellow. He stared at Lucas, his mouth curling into a smile around the wadding that filled his mouth, preventing him from uttering any sound he might use as magic.

A guard of stone men ringed the Shrieker. That was the name of the men who had volunteered to defend Fearnot's walls had given themselves.

"You have seen the Council vote. I command you to stand aside!" Asher shouted.

The stone men ignored him, spears blocking his path. Hayden commanded them. But as a man, they looked at Lucas.

"No, Asher! Are you insane?!" Lucas thundered.

Asher had a triumphant grin on his face. "We voted, Lucas. Tobias and Earl took my side. The Council has chosen Ademar to be our intermediary. He has already told me that his master has no quarrel with us."

"You've spoken to him?!" Lucas exclaimed in horror. "You could have killed us all, you fool!"

Asher scoffed. "We are all still here, aren't we? He voluntarily allowed himself to be gagged again afterward. They sent him to us to negotiate. Atramen wants the thief who stole from him in Argent. Items of great power which are in the wrong hands…"

Lucas couldn't believe what he was hearing. Asher rambled as he spoke. Lucas saw Seth and Avery nodding. Tobias and Earl looked more uncertain.

He glared at the Shrieker. How long had he spoken to Asher for? Were Seth and Avery there when it happened?

"You are not yourself, Asher Lawless," Lucas whispered. "I believe you are under a spell cast by the Prisoner." He turned to Seth and Avery.

"Were you there when Asher spoke to the Prisoner?"

"Yes, listen to him, Lucas. He makes sense!" Avery replied urgently.

"How long can we hold out for, anyway? We need to make peace!" Seth said at the same time.

Lucas nodded. "That's what I thought."

"Hayden, order your men to release Ademar!" Asher instructed. "It is the will of the Council…!"

"The Council is disbanded," Lucas told him flatly.

All stared at him.

"Lucas? There has been a Council governing Fearnot for generations…." Hayden began.

"Now, we see the truth!" Asher crowd. "Lucas wants power for himself!"

A thunder of boots filled the Hall. Lucas glanced over his shoulder. The storm riders had arrived. A dozen young men and women crowded into the Hall, each carrying a drawn sword. Beyond them, he saw a crowd gathering, including members of the Women's Circle.

"Take the prisoner back to his cell," Lucas ordered. The stone men guard did not hesitate.

"Avery Shoreman, Seth Markshem, Asher Lawless. You are under arrest. Jan, they need to be held separately from the Prisoner, and no one sees them unless you have a direct order from me. Understand?" Lucas knew his voice was cold. He had learned the tone from seeing Jerad giving orders in times of trouble. It worked. Jan counted off storm riders, and they seized the three. Two women succeeded in barging their way into the hall.

Ivy Greenford looked from her husband, Hayden, to Lucas as though trying to decide which caused the trouble.

"Will one of you tell me what is going on here?"

"In my absence, these three were going to release the Prisoner. Did the Women's Circle know?"

"No, of course not!" Lilly Hawskmar stood at Ivy's side, and the two were often inseparable. She was tall and waspish, in contrast to Ivy's rotund figure. "We would never have agreed to that. Tobias, what have you men done?!"

"The Council is in a state of disarray. I cannot trust it any longer. I have dissolved it. Until Jerad returns to take charge, I will govern Fearnot."

All stared at Lucas. Fearnot had never, in memory or history, had a king or a chieftain of any kind. A Women's Circle had always supported a Council of Nine.

Ivy's green eyes blazed, her round face reddening. "You can't…!" she started, but the sudden tolling of bells interrupted her.

"That's the south wall alarm!" Hayden said just as a red-faced, out-of-breath stone man burst into the hall. He looked taken aback momentarily at the crowd of armed storm riders. Then his eyes alighted on Hayden and Lucas.

"Sirs!" He shouted. Lucas recognized Glyn Waken; a man old enough to be his father. "The enemy is attacking the south wall. There are hundreds of them!"

CHAPTER 13:
HEALING EVIL

There was no warning of the attack until the first scream tore the night apart. Alecyn came awake from a fitful sleep. They had camped in a hollow below the ridge of a hill. The hill slopes were bare of trees, providing an unencumbered view of anyone attempting to approach the camp. A ring of Nelim sentries hid among the rocks that littered the landscape while the rest tried to sleep as best they could, wrapped up against the biting wind. They doused the cookfire as soon as it was no longer needed.

Alecyn huddled back-to-back with Mendel for warmth. Jerad lay facing her. She had felt his eyes on her long after she had closed hers.

The first scream was from the Nelim. It degenerated rapidly into terrible gurgling. Then next was a Mute, unleashing its unearthly noise. As it washed over her, Alecyn felt the power of it as a sick feeling in her stomach. Mendel covered his ears, squeezing his eyes shut tight. Then, the air was alive with war cries and shouted orders. Vanja's booming voice above all. He was taking his turn on the sentry line tonight, and his reactions were instant.

Jerad was only a heartbeat slower. The Noise from the Mutes had barely begun when he was on his feet, rousing the rest of the camp.

Alecyn stood, going to the edge of the hollow to see for herself. Jerad ordered her back, but she ignored him. Mendel was at her side, holding the cloth-wrapped bundle that was the Fragment. It never left his sight, though Alecyn had not brought herself to touch it again. She saw black shapes spilling out of the trees and racing up the hillside in the moonlight. They leaped, arcing high into the air and covering dozens of yards. The sentries stood, awaiting the charge with long spears. Behind them, archers sought the moving shadows against the pale hillside, using arrows that screamed and whined as they flew.

"What should we do?" Mendel asked anxiously.

This wasn't the first skirmish they had found themselves in, but to Alecyn, it looked to be the biggest. She found it impossible to calculate the number of Mutes that stormed up the open hillside towards them. Before now, it had been small, with mostly human patrols with one or two mutes.

"We stay out of the way and be ready to help the wounded," Alecyn told him.

"Do you not think the Fragment…?" Mendel began, but Alecyn wouldn't hear of it.

"No, Mendel! I told you."

She could not look at the Fragment since they had left the Heart. It terrified her still. The impressive power the object held. But what frightened her was that she couldn't avoid using it for much longer. They had been heading west through the highland forests for a week now. She had tried to take them all instantly to Fearnot using her power. Looking at a crude map drawn on the ground of its location. She had tried to picture a safe place and allow their need to direct her power. Nothing worked. And with each failure, she saw the dark looks passing among the Nelim and the growing desperation on Jerad's face. She felt the siren call of the Waeferen artifact.

Mutes were clashing now with Nelim. There was a dull, crunching sound as the armored creatures thudded into the spears and shields of the defenders. A second ring of warriors formed higher up the hill than the first, led by Jerad. They rushed in to attack any Mutes whose bounds carried them over the first line. Alecyn's heart was in her mouth whenever she saw him bound into the fray, whip bow lashing out. She saw a Nelim beside him fall, clutching his leg. Although ready to leap away, Jerad employed his whip to catch the Mute by the throat, causing it to lose its balance. The wounded Nelim slashed with its hind limbs and severed the creature's head.

"Come on, Mendel! We are going to help!"

Alecyn dashed down the slope to the Nelim, who was being helped away from the battle by Jerad. Mendel and Alecyn took the burden from him.

"We will take care of him!" Alecyn told him firmly. Jerad nodded and ran back into the fight.

It was a pattern that was to be repeated. Alecyn had lost track of time when she realized the attack was over. She had lost herself in her own battle. She and Mendel had run from wounded to wounded. She embraced the power each time, listening to the Song of the injured Nelim before her and pouring her energy into it. She attempted to heal all the injuries, but she couldn't heal all of them.

"Are they gone?" She asked when she realized for the first time that no more noise was filling the air.

"Chased away!" Vanja crowded.

"For now," Jerad said grimly. "This was a test."

"What do you mean?" Alecyn asked.

"They came on in waves. I have never seen a Mute with enough self-control to resist an attack. There was a human commanding them, a Shrieker. He or she wanted to see how strong a group we are. And how strong of a sorcerer you are," he said, looking at Alecyn. "Now they have an idea. The next time they hit us, the Shrieker will join the fight.

"Human, my warriors have no equal in this world. But I tell you this, we cannot hold an open hilltop against another force like that. Not if they have magic to back them." Vanja towered over Alecyn. Jerad interposed himself.

"Easy, there, Vanja. She is doing her best. We would not have survived tonight if not for her healing."

"If we face a Shrieker in battle, we need a sorcerer to counter them. Someone who is prepared to fight." He looked at Jerad challengingly. "Or we will all die."

"Back off, Vanja!" Jerad growled, his fists clenching.

Mendel took Alecyn's arm, pulling her aside. He said nothing, but Alecyn felt him press the Fragment against her arm. There was no choice. She fought down the dread that rose in the pit of her stomach.

"How long do we have?" She asked Jerad.

"Probably until tomorrow night. Mutes have no problem with light or dark, but the Shrieker will know they have an advantage over us at night."

"I need to rest before I can try this," Alecyn said. She tried to keep the shaking from her voice.

"You have done enough for one night, Alecyn," Jerad said kindly. "Rest up for now."

Vanja growled something in the Nelim tongue, and Alecyn's temper snapped. It was partly exhaustion, partly the constant gnawing fear of a journey through a hostile country. She remembered an old man she had treated once, his constant carping and complaining. His attitude of entitlement prevented any sense of gratitude. Alecyn had never had the courage to tell him to his face what she thought of him. She had smiled politely and kept her professional veneer.

"What is your problem, Vanja?" she demanded. "Did I not heal everyone I could? Did we not put ourselves in harm's way enough times or send enough of your warriors back to the lines whole after wounds that should have killed them? What more do you want from me?"

Vanja's chest heaved. His face darkened, hind limbs arching high above his shoulders.

"I live to fight the Silence, human. You are a sorceress and can help that fight. I do not understand why you will not. When one of my warriors refuses to fight, it is because he is afraid. And we cast him out. We wonder what keeps you from using your power as you should."

"Without her efforts, your warriors would be dead or wounded!" Jerad interjects.

"I know this. I am not blind. I still wonder what she is holding back and why."

Alecyn fought to control her anger. She had never liked the soldier's mentality. Whether it was the politician who advocated the bombing of cities to punish a rogue state or the constant glorification of warrior heroes in every aspect of the culture she had been born into, she would not mirror the aggression that Vanja was showing.

"I took an oath. That I would save life and never take it. I take that oath seriously and will die before I break it."

Alecyn turned and walked away, Mendel at her side. Vanja threw up his arms and stalked away in the opposite direction. Jerad followed, but one of Vanja's lieutenants, Idrasi, caught his arm. The Nelim's face rippled with color. It tucked its hind limbs back out of sight.

"Tell her we do not think of her as a coward. We all saw her and the mystic during the fight. They acted with great courage." Idrasi fingered a thin white line down one arm, all that remained of a wound a Mute had opened to the bone. "We are all grateful. Vanja does not know how to express himself unless it is shouting."

Jerad thumped the Nelim's shoulder with his knuckles, a gesture of comradeship. The return gesture would have been enough to knock him onto his heels had he not braced himself for it. He walked back up the hillside, among the rocks and Mute bodies. Rounding a sizable boulder, he found Alecyn and Mendel crouching on the ground, examining one body.

Alecyn looked up. Her eyes had dark smudges, but a glint of fire still shone through.

"The Nelim wanted to let the two of you know they recognized your courage today. No one thinks either of you is a coward."

"I'm sure I am," Mendel said, looking at Alecyn. "Had I the choice, I would not have been able to stop myself from running."

Jerad crouched across the Mute body. "You had the choice. It just would not have done you much good. I am glad you are with us." He looked at Mendel as he said it but was clearly talking to Alecyn. Mendel flushed bright blue, clearly uncomfortable.

"Thank you for standing up for me, though, Jerad," Alecyn said. "I always feel safer with you around." Their eyes met and held for a long moment. Mendel looked from one to the other, his color brightening by the second. Alecyn tore her eyes away first.

"I will miss you when I find the way home, Jerad," she said hurriedly.

"As will I. When you leave... as will I." Jerad replied.

"What has you so interested in this offal?" he said, indicating the body before them.

Alecyn looked at it blankly for a moment, and then realization dawned on her.

"Yes. As we passed the bodies, I thought I could detect them at the edge of hearing. A tune, a melody. It is different each time but similar. By the same composer. I got the same theme from you. But not Mendel. These Mutes used to be human, didn't they?" It wasn't a question. Alecyn was certain.

Jerad looked over the black armor plates, oozing with viscous liquid. Grimacing, he pulled at the two halves of the faceplate, prying it open. Inside was a human face. Its features were becoming blurred, as though it was lacking definition. The face had no clear features; the nose seemed to merge with it, and all hair disappeared as if the flesh was melting wax. He let the faceplate close, wiping his hands on the grass.

"Yes, it used to be human."

"How long ago would you say this person was... changed?" Alecyn asked, swallowing with revulsion.

Jerad shook his head. "I could not say, but the features are still there. Just about a few months?"

"And I can still hear humanity in it? If I can hear its Song, even a fragment, I can heal it. Or at least see where healing might be done."

Jerad stared at her. "You can't be serious. This, this... thing is not human anymore. It's a monster. You can't heal it."

"If I can strengthen the human element of the song and restore it, then why won't that restore the human part of its body?"

"Because the human parts have been dissolved, eaten," Jerad said. "There is nothing left of the person that was."

"Yes, there is. I could hear its song. And I can hear it. I can heal it."

"But not now, we agreed." Mendel reminded her gently. "Now we rest, and later, we try to transport everyone to a place of safety. We decided."

Alecyn nodded distractedly. "Yes, Mendel. But I will try this. Jerad, is it possible to capture a Mute alive?"

"Alive! Great Song!!" Jerad sat back on his heels. "Do you have any idea how dangerous that would be?!"

"No, not really," Alecyn admitted. "But I need a live one. Jerad, trust me!"

Jerad looked into her shining eyes. "I will try." He spoke.

Alecyn's smile lit up her face. She leaned forward impulsively and kissed his cheek. There was a heartbeat, and then both pulled back. Alecyn was scarlet. Jerad was on his feet as though stung.

"I need to see to the sentry line." He blurted, and then he was off down the hill.

****

The day passed uneventfully. The Nelim waited watchfully for an attack, which did not come. Alecyn tried to sleep but only dozed. While awake, she and Mendel discussed how they might work the song to transport the group to safety. Now she sat, Mendel across from her, the cloth-wrapped bundle of the song fragment between them. She did not want to reveal it to the Nelim. It would lead to too many questions about how she got it. It would also increase the pressure on her to use it. To direct its power to wipe out Atramen and his army. Alecyn could never bring herself to do that, especially now that she could see a way of restoring humanity to those he had changed.

Alecyn closed her eyes. She sifted through the multitude of music she could hear all around her. The Songs of the Nelim, Jerad, the earth, the discordant chaos of the Mutes. Over it all was the glorious symphony of the Song Fragment. She embraced it, opening her mouth and allowing it to sing through her. The melody was wordless, and her voice was an instrument producing pure music. She felt the lure of the raw power that existed all around her. In her companions. In the world itself. She could draw enough to achieve anything. But she knew it would be wrong. It would change her. She could still feel the exaltation of limitless power in the moment before she had struck down Erevar. That terrible, dark version of herself still lurked within.

She focused on the simple map diagram of Fearnot that Jerad had drawn for her. Alecyn had memorized every line. It wasn't just so that she could take them there. It was his home. She wanted to know and was fascinated to see the place where he had existed before she had met him.

Stop it! She was going home! Home! There was no place for him there.

Alecyn reached within for the power to pour through the Song. It was hard. There was resistance, a black fatigue that threatened to overwhelm her. She fought through it. Then, the world suddenly rushed past her. It was like she was moving rapidly. The landscape blurred around her.

But she could feel the ground beneath her. As she tried to keep the image of Fearnot uppermost, a haze of images assaulted her. Places she didn't recognize, people she had never seen before. She saw a city with a towering mountain rising from its heart. She saw a man with white hair and eyes who looked at her in astonishment. He had been looking up at a wall inscribed with wheels and cogs.

She saw a cat, its face almost touching hers. She felt its surprise and then, briefly, pure joy before it disappeared.

"Eevee!" Alecyn shouted.

Then there was darkness and silence. Eyes became accustomed to the gloom, and a shape appeared, outlined by starlight. It was an enormous feline figure, eyes shining like torches in the gloom. There were many figures, many bright eyes.

"Hello again, human." purred Krissker.

CHAPTER 14:

THE PRIDE AND THE PLAN

There was a silence which screamed of human and Nelim shock. Then the hiss of a struck flint and firelight flared. Alecyn saw stone walls rising to an open night sky framed by a gaping circular hole. The walls curved and revealed a ruined tower. She and her group were all where they had been, but the world had changed. In front of her was a giant cat's massive black and white bulk. Others stood all around, dozens of them amongst the Nelim. She felt Mendel's grip tighten painfully on her arm, and a panicked whimper came from him.

Jerad crouched a few feet away, looking around him in shock. Alecyn looked up into the eyes of the figure which had spoken. It had directed its words at Jerad, but now he turned to look at her.

She got to her feet, suppressing a sense of vertigo at the height that this creature still towered above her.

"Hello. I am Alecyn Johnsenn," she said, fighting to keep her voice trembling.

"I know," the cat purred. "I am Krissker, of the Sunmane Pride of the Free Kajani. The little mother showed us your face and gave us your name. Your warrior found you then."

"My warrior?" Alecyn looked over at Jerad, who was regaining his composure and walking to stand beside her. The Nelim watched the cats wearily, with hind limbs twitching and arched high while still holding the deadly blades low to their backs. Vanja, on seeing Jerad move, walked confidently through the cats to join him. A hissing snarl was the only warning he got. Claws extended a furred limb thrust in his path.

He froze, and with a twitch of his hand, a dozen Nelim blades scythed high into the air. A yowling screech rose from the Kajani. Krissker whirled, roaring a long stream of indecipherable sounds. His golden eyes fixed on Vanja.

"There will be no Hunts here, Nelim. And no Kajani hides for Nelim cloaks, either. You travel with two friends from the Free Kajani. You are in no danger from us. But you will be if those blades don't vanish. Now!"

Alecyn winced. If anyone was incapable of responding to shouted orders, it was Vanja.

"Vanja! I know these Kajani. They mean us no harm." Jerad said.

"Humans, the Nelim and the Kajani are enemies by blood. But I have no desire to die in battle with any but the minions of the Silence." Vanja barked an order in the Nelim language, and his warriors slowly sheathed their bladed limbs. Vanja stalked towards Alecyn and Jerad, brushing past the Kajani that stood in his way and topped him by a head in height. A wave of purring growls followed him. Alecyn growled in exasperation.

"Kr... Krissker?" She hesitated over the name, hoping she had got it right. "You seem to know me, but we have never met."

"The Little Mother showed us your face in a vision. She sent us to help this human, to send him to your side."

Alecyn looked at Jerad in confusion. There was something on his face: sympathy.

"What, Little Mother?"

Krissker shrugged. "A being of great power. I called her Little Mother because she was like a mother. One must not cross her. One who is older than all around her and demands obedience. But she was small. Like us, but small." He held paws the size of dinner plates a short distance apart.

"Eevee sent Krissker to Lucus and I when the Kajani hunted us. She brought me to you," Jerad told her.

"Eevee…" Alecyn whispered.

"Krissker. The Little Mother is... she didn't make it. The Enemy killed her." Jerad said to Krissker, putting a hand on Alecyn's shoulder.

"No," whispered Alecyn.

"No, human." Krissker rumbled. "You are mistaken. The Little Mother has not left us."

Alecyn's head whipped up, eyes blazing. "Eevee is alive! Have you seen her? How do you know?!" Excitedly, she had gripped Krissker's forearm, and he gently placed a paw on her hand. It swamped her own hand, smothering it under a thick layer of black and white fur.

"Her spirit touched me. I call her the Little Mother, and you Eevee, a being that my people know well. Her spirit touched me, and I have felt that touch since."

"Where?"

Krissker rolled his golden eyes and flicked his head back in two quick snaps. She didn't understand the meaning of the gesture, but his words were clear. "In no place. In here." He tapped his chest. "A month ago, she passed through my dreams. She was searching as though lost. I called out to her, and she heard me, but something carried her beyond me." His shoulders heaved. "We are not as familiar with the ghost plains as your Nelim friends."

Another Kajani spoke. "They hide in the ghost realm and leave the world that gave them birth to the Bitterbloods."

Krissker looked at Vanja, and black lips parted to reveal a hint of white teeth. Vanja's chest heaved, but he returned the stare without expression.

The other Nelim looked at their leader.

"I will not start the fight, cat," Vanja hissed. "And know this. The days of the mystics are done. The Nelim has returned to take back what the mystics abandoned. We will fight."

"Then we welcome you. And we will see who their ancestors are more honored in battle, you, or us."

Krisskers' mouth widened further to reveal the full extent of fangs a hand's width long.

Alecyn reached out to grab a handful of the big cat's fur. It felt matted and greasy, but she tugged forcefully to turn Krissker's head to her.

"Listen to me! Eevee told you about me?"

Krissker's eyes widened, and he raised a massive paw in surprise. But Alecyn refused to be deterred. She gripped her flute in her free hand. Krissker's eyes darted to it, then to her face, then to Jerad. She thought he looked worried.

"Better answer her questions, Krissker. You know what she is." Jerad told him.

Krissker took her hand, gently trying to disengage it. Alecyn tightened her grip and lifted the flute in warning. "She told me your name and that you were a powerful sorceress, that you had the power to drive the Silence from the world. That is why I was prepared to kill my own to help this one find you."

"That's right, Krissker. I am powerful enough to escape from Argent being undetected by Atramen. I saved these Nelim from the Black Hand and could destroy his entire army without taking a single life. Do you want to live in a world where there is no longer a need to fight and kill?"

Krissker's eyes narrowed to fiery slits. "The Free Kajani wish to live as our ancestors did, as hunters. Not warriors."

Vanja snorted, and Alecyn shot him with a daggered look. "You and all your brothers will have chances to get yourself killed if that is all you care about, Vanja. The truly brave here will rebuild this world when your battle ends." Vanja's skin flashed dark blue, and he lunged for her. Alecyn was ready even before Krissker pushed her back as he and Jerad moved to block Vanja's path. Alecyn put the flute to her lips and played.

The tune she chose was 'Sweeping the Halls,' a jaunty Irish song whose merry melody hid a darkness in its words. She knew that her Voice was the most powerful form of magic she had, but she didn't trust that she could summon enough of the power from within to put it to use. So, she fell back on the instrument which had served her so well in this world. She visualized Vanja, his lethal hind limbs twisted and knotted above his head uselessly. The tune wafted through the air, Kajani's ears pricking up. Some Nelim had also drawn their blades. Alecyn caught all of them with her eye. She turned a slow circle, always playing and noting those ready to fight.

In each case, those blade limbs twitched and then stretched straight up, twisting about each other. A group stood behind the Nelim, whom Alecyn often saw standing at Vanja's shoulder. Idrasi, she had heard him called. None had their weapons drawn. Idrasi stood with arms firmly folded as Vanja's lunge stopped short. Alecyn put down the flute, stepped around Jerad, and faced the Nelim leader.

"I would have said your aggression comes from grief at the destruction of your home. But I think you don't mourn the Heart's burning, do you?" Alecyn's heart was beating hard. She had stood up to the giant Krissker because of her shock at the thought that Eevee was still alive. This was different. Vanja reminded her strongly of the politicians she had become used to seeing on TV, those who advocated the bombing strikes and the invasions against those they described as rogue states or terrorists. She had wanted to scream at them. It would be the civilians who died, not the rogue leaders, not the orchestrators of terror. She knew the chaos of an emergency room and now knew the horror of a battlefield. How could anyone relish that so much? "You wanted it. Because it lets you do what you have always wanted. Fight, kill, and then die. Did you want it, Vanja?"

The Nelim paled. He became as white as Mendel. His hind limbs relaxed, still hopelessly twisted around each other. He stepped back from Alecyn.

"I fight to avenge my people." Then he turned away. Alecyn could feel her racing heart. She felt as though she had been holding her breath. Jerad stared at her with wide eyes and a half smile creeping across his face.

Mendel clapped, though he stopped in a flush of purple as Nelim and Kajani's eyes fixed on him.

"I am glad Eevee is still alive, Krissker. She is my best friend."

"You are strange indeed, human," Krissker said, a new respect in his voice. "Not least to claim a friendship with one such as her. I would not have believed it possible."

"Such as she?" Alecyn asked. "What is she?"

"The ones you call Waeferen," Krissker replied. "They raised us from our primitive ancestors, gave us the fire of intelligence. Cubs have passed the knowledge of their spirit form from cub to adult through every den and pride.

Eevee was one of the Waeferen. One of the legendary races who had built the gateways, who had transcribed the Great Song itself. Had she ever just been a cat? Had she chosen Alecyn to come here? Was anything that happened to her just an accident or a part of some plan? Alecyn's head whirled. But the knowledge felt right. Something had clicked home in her mind. Instinctively, she knew Krissker was right.

"Alecyn?" Jerad was by her side. "Are you well?" he asked solicitously.

"Yes…" Alecyn began. "Yes. I am fine. Tired is all, Jerad." She turned back to Krissker.

"No matter. Where exactly have I brought us, Krissker?"

The Kajani looked uncertain briefly, eyes darting to Jerad and even Vanja before returning to Alecyn. She kept her look level and was determined not to look at Jerad for support. She wanted Krissker to see her as the leader.

She was tired of trying to steer warriors bent on killing themselves. The Kajani knew her as a sorceress. She wanted to keep up the momentum. Krissker inclined his head slightly, a huge pink tongue flicking up to lick his nose. His jaws then opened wide in a terrifying and cavernous yawn. Alecyn hoped these were signs of submission and not escalating aggression.

"Very well, my... lady," Krissker said. "This was a human construction, built in the loop of a river about a two-day run from one of your... cities."

There was immense distaste in his voice at the word. "We saw it under attack from the Bitterbloods and tried to come to the defenders' aid. Despite being late, we eliminated those who attacked. However, we came upon a large force when we left here and were forced to seek refuge within the walls. We are now trapped, like those we have tried to help. The humans here fought under the banner of a white stag on a green background."

"I think I know it," Jerad said. "The banner of the Tredell Lords. The line ended generations ago, but they held a castle on the Tar. Long ago, they redirected the river to surround it on three sides. But there is no city anywhere near it."

"The city is where the Bitterbloods have driven all the humans."

Krissker continued. "They make it a city, I think. Many of the giant birds come and go from there."

"Stormbirds!" Jerad said excitedly. "It must be Fearnot! When did you last see it, Krissker? Are they holding out?"

"They were seven suns ago, human. That was the last time we saw the place."

Alecyn took Jerad's hand and squeezed. The hope that had lit his face at Krissker's words sent a thrill through her.

"How many do you have with you, Krissker?" Jerad demanded.

"Not enough to fight through the creatures that encircle us human. Even with your Nelim allies. We hold this place, that is all."

"What kind of force holds you?" came a Nelim voice. It was Idrasi, stepping forward and pointedly ignoring Vanja. "What do we face?"

"Bitterbloods and humans. Five hundred," Krissker replied.

"No Shriekers?" The Nelim asked, making a gesture as though to cover his face.

"The Faceless?" Krissker replied. "No, our scouts spotted a large party heading towards us, Faceless leading Bitterbloods, not long after we came here. We readied ourselves to meet our ancestors. But they turned back, leaving the Bitterbloods to fight alone. We do not know why. I think just one of the Faceless could reduce these old walls. I believe none of them have joined those who surround the city either. I wonder where they fight."

Jerad was about to speak, but Alecyn refused to allow the surrounding men—she included Kajani and the Nelim in that description—to turn the conversation back to war.

"That's good, Krissker. But I can end this war with no more bloodshed."

All eyes were on her.

****

An icy wind stroked her hair. She pulled the thick cloak one of the Kajani had given her tight around herself. She stood on the castle's walls, looking across the river at the forest surrounding them as far as the eye could see. Columns of smoke rose in places all around them.

Jerad had pointed them out as cook fires, and Krissker had growled that he could smell Kajani's flesh burning on those fires. Alecyn had come up to the castle battlements to feel the fresh air. She wanted a moment of peace before what was about to happen. Mendel wandered the courtyard below, professing a dislike of walking along the high stone walls.

"I find it hard to trust anything so high from the ground to hold me up that isn't living." He had told her.

She was glad. It was her first time alone with her thoughts since the Heart. The first time, she hadn't felt the constant fear of a sudden attack. She knew their enemies were out there, the Mutes. But Krissker and his pride had carved out a buffer around the castle and held it. The attacks still came, but during the day, at least the castle and its surroundings were quiet.

She had outlined her plan to Krissker, Jerad, Idrasi, and Mendel. The others assembled nearer to listen intently until both Idrasi and Krissker issued directives to their respective warriors to proceed with their duties. Soon, Nelim and Kajani had stationed themselves about the castle's defenses. It had given Alecyn time to work on her plan. Adding to it as she went. It could work. It would work! Then came the day and a night with Mendel trying to understand how to use the Fragment to execute the plan. She was tired, her head ached from hours spent concentrating, but she also felt exhilarated. And, she realized, home had never seemed so far away. Was she becoming Alecyn the Sorceress? What was happening to Alecyn Johnsenn?

The terrible noise of a Mute rose above the natural forest sounds. A roaring snarl of Kajani followed it. So soon? She turned away from the forest. In the courtyard below, Mendel had stopped pacing and looked up at her. The Fragment clutched to his chest. As Alecyn walked to the wooden steps that led down from the battlements, the gates swung open, and a sprinting auburn-furred Kajani streaked into the courtyard. By the time she reached the flagstone floor, Krissker was striding out.

He looked at her. "It is time, my lady. We have captured a live Mute."

CHAPTER 15:
THE BATTLE FOR FEARNOT

Lucas was racing for the aviary. Around him, people were milling in confusion. Over everything were the warning bells and horns that told of an attack. He was aware of angry shouts directed at his back by Ivy.

"You can't just run off!" yelled Ivy.

The storm riders ran around him, buckling coats and helmets as they sprinted toward their mounts. If the Mutes were attacking, their place was in the air. The cold, inhuman voice at the back of his mind calmly told him that his place was not among the flyers this time. He ignored it. Now, all he wanted was the simplicity of the fight. He didn't want the politics of the Council, the fuzzy gray decisions that lacked clarity. No right or wrong answer. Around him, he could see members of the Women's Circle beginning to gain control over the confusion. They directed people to the Great Hall, where a group of older stone men formed. The women, the children, and the elderly were supposed to take shelter there, at the heart of Fearnot and furthest from the walls. He was glad Ivy and the other women were there to take charge.

He reached the hilltop and looked down the hill towards the walls. A sea of black was spilling out of the forest to the east. They were massing but had not yet charged. Men were atop the walls, more climbing the boulders used to create the makeshift fortification. Readying themselves. He vaulted over the fence surrounding the stormbird pens and was about to head towards Cullhain when someone firmly grabbed his collar, stopping him.

Hayden held him in an unshakeable grip.

"Not you, Lucas." he said.

"What are you doing, Hayden? I need to get up there!"

"Not anymore you don't. We need you on the ground."

Lucas rounded on the older man. "I am the best flyer in the Southlands and Cullhain the best stormbird. And no one else can ride him but me."

"Then you need to look at training that bird to accept someone else as his rider. We can't afford to lose you."

Lucas struggled, an icy fear knotting his stomach. He couldn't let his stormrider's face battle alone. While they risked their lives, he couldn't stay on the ground. He wasn't a general!

"Look, son. It goes with the territory. I know you didn't look for this, but it's found you, and do you know what? Without you, this place would have been overrun a long time ago.

Lucas stopped struggling. "This is a mistake, I promise you."

Hayden slowly released his grip. "I don't think so... sir." Lucas looked up at him, startled. "Get used to that, sir," Hayden said with a rueful grin.

Lucas nodded. "We need our birds in the air. And..." He paused for a moment. What needed to happen next? He needed to know what was happening. He couldn't see the entire perimeter walls from here. For that, he needed scouts. He needed orders carried to those scouts. He needed someone to carry orders, to write them as he spoke them.

"Lucas!" Adellin came running up the hill, a group of girls and older boys following her. "Lucas, what can we do? These boys are too young to fight, but we can do something."

Lucas had been about to order them to the Great Hall, but he stopped.

"Hayden, I need charcoal and parchment to write with. Adellin, you are all going to be runners. You will need to take orders through the city for me and bring the news back. Horses would be good…"

He lost himself in a maze of orders. He remained on the hilltop. Someone brought him a table piled with parchment and charcoal sticks to mark it with. A string of teenage boys and girls soon ran or rode at his behest, clutching rolled parchments. Lucas tried to keep the entire city in mind, piecing together what he could see from the hilltop with what others told him of where he couldn't see. It wasn't good. The Mutes had charged. The first time they had attacked was during the day. They had swarmed up the eastern walls and over them. Lines of stone men had charged into the fray while bowmen took control of the wall and rooftops, picking off flying Mutes with screaming arrows. But for every black shape that fell, pierced through an open faceplate, two more were leaping to mount the walls.

Another attack had begun from the north, where a trench carried water from the Tar to create a moat. Archers on the far side maintained volley after volley into the black ranks, standing their ground bravely, only to be overrun. Parven had taken command of the defenders from the White Coast, north of Ghoul's Creek. Lucas was told he had rallied the stone men who had fled when the Mutes scaled the walls, leading them back and momentarily pushing the black tide back into the moat. Lucas sent out runners to reinforce

Parven's men. But it meant that the south, which hadn't yet faced an attack, would see a decrease in strength.

The stormbirds were everywhere. Scouring the walls, they circled Fearnot and came away with talons and beaks full of Mutes. They collected squads of stone men and placed them onto the walls where they were most needed. They carried vats of flaming lamp oil, stoked with glee by Lily Hawksmar and a cadre of women on the other side of the Aviary to Lucas' command post. She cheered on every departed flight, carrying a sloshing wooden barrel to drop onto the enemy.

He could see what was happening and knew he was the only one. Everyone was so focused on their small part of the battle. None, but he could see its entirety. And what he could see was that they couldn't hope to win. This was the last battle. The enemy had harassed them, driven the people of the Southland into one place, and was now dealing with the final blow. Kill everyone all at once. Lucas only wondered why this all-powerful sorceress had not used magic.

There was a sudden whoosh of flames, and for a moment, Lucas thought Atramen had finally thrown his powers into the fray. He turned in his seat and saw that someone had brought down a stormbird carrying one of Lily's flaming vats. It had crashed into houses, and its burden exploded across the rooftops. Fire now raged in the streets east of Fearnot behind the walls. The fire spread rapidly, consuming the tents and timber buildings in the eastern half of the city that accommodated the refugees. Before long, the men on the walls would find themselves cut off.

"Great Song! Not that." It was Ivy's voice. "Not fire on top of everything else. Lucas, we must organize anyone who isn't fighting to stop the fire before it burns the town down from under us." She had come up the hill from the green where the wounded were being tended beside the Harp. She had rolled up her sleeves, and her hands looked pink and scrubbed.

"No," said Lucas as a vision unfolded before his eyes. "We need to stoke it higher."

"What are you talking about, man?!" Ivy barked.

"The Mutes are over the eastern walls and will soon be across the river. We will pull everyone back to this side of the fire and use it as our eastern wall. Blake!" He called out to Blake, who was checking on a returned Stormbird. He hurried over to Lucas.

"I need as many stormbirds as we can spare to pick up whatever rocks they can tear loose from the eastern walls and drop them north and south of that fire. Then we will drop any of Lily's lamp oil that we still have left into it to stoke it up. We need it burning higher than even a Mute can leap, understand!"

He had long ago lost any self-consciousness at barking orders to men twice his age and seniority on the Council. Blake listened intently and, with a nod, was running back to his charges, already calling on Stormriders. Lucas scanned the eastern horizon with the telescope someone had brought him. He didn't know who, only that Adellin had pressed it into his hands as he had been sending runners to find men to break up houses for the wood, to supply Master Avrar the fletcher. He had been dimly aware that Adellin had also pressed food and drink into his hands. Though it was still strewn across the table, half consumed and forgotten.

The sun was sitting low now, above the licking flames that cut a swathe a mile wide across what had been homes. Stormbirds were tearing at the walls, their riders shooting frantically at marauding Mutes. Rocks were already in place, impeding the fire's progress to the north and south as planned. But it was taking a toll on the stormbirds themselves, as they were completely unprotected as they landed and tried to rip mortar rocks off the walls. To the north, a chain of spearmen stood in a line that bowed inwards under the weight of charging human troops. They had come from the trees behind the onslaught of Mutes, wearing black armor and horned helms. The walls had all fallen, and now the spearmen made their line amongst the houses, archers on the rooftops above them. A lone stormbird circled and dove to cover them from the air.

They were ready to crack. To the east, men fought to contain groups of Mutes and humans trying to get around the sides of the fire. If they got loose in the city, there would be carnage. Everything was spinning out of his control.

"General Haverford!" came a small voice. Lucas looked for it, finding a boy of only ten at his elbow. He clutched a parchment in a grubby fist.

"Sir, Master Tobias says that he is under attack. He needs more men!"

"I have no more to give him," Lucas said numbly, taking the parchment on which Tobias had scrawled his desperate plea. Tobias was at the south wall. Lucas didn't know what to do. There was nothing else he could do. They were lost. He looked down at the boy, who was waiting for the orders he was to carry back to Tobias. There was fear in the boy's face and trust. He looked at Lucas with absolute conviction. He knew Lucas would somehow save the day.

"I must do something. We are dead anyway if I don't," Lucas mumbled.

"Adellin. Adellin, where are you?"

Adellin had found fresh food and a steaming tankard from somewhere and had been hurrying up the hill to him. "Never mind that now! I need the Prisoner up here now!" She gaped at him.

"Lucas, you can't be thinking..."

"I am. It is the only chance we have left. There must be a reason Atramen didn't just send his Shriekers to smash Fearnot into pieces around us. Why didn't he produce all that magic he used to take Argent? Why? What are we missing here? I must know."

"But you said yourself. If that... that creature is loose, it will kill us all."

"We are dead anyway by the next morning. We can't hold on. Please Adellin."

Lucas watched her go and then raised his eyes to look out over the beleaguered city. It had welcomed him. Fearnot had become a home to him that Ghoul's Creek had never been. He wouldn't let it go, even if he had to make a deal with the devil to save it.

CHAPTER 16:
ATRAMEN

It took three Kajani, each holding a thick hawser of rope so taut that it hummed. Between them, lashed from chest to toe, was a Mute. Its head lashed, its face plate opened, and it emitted noise. All the Kajani had dark blood staining the fur around their ears. Alecyn and those within the castle had fashioned ear protectors out of wads of cloth, but the Kajani refused.

Their heads bowed, they cringed each time the Mute opened its faceplate and screamed its defiance as though they were being physically struck.

"Into the center!" Jerad yelled over his own earplugs. "As far from the walls as we can!"

The Kajani continued to howl. A chorus of howling shrieks came from outside, and a group of Kajani tore through the open gate. Each carried a Nelim warrior on its back. As Alecyn reached Mendel, grasping his hand, she noted that of the Nelim riders, there was one warrior loyal to Idrasi.

"Vanja! For Noise's sake! We need a perimeter guard on the walls!" Jerad was looking towards the open-roofed keep, the part of the castle that Alecyn had transported them all to. Since his public humiliation days before, Vanja and his most loyal followers had not stirred themselves from there. Alecyn opened her mouth to say something to Jerad but felt Mendel squeeze her hand urgently. She looked up at him and knew the tense urgency on his face. It told her she was allowing herself to be distracted.

She nodded and kept silent as Jerad stalked towards the steps leading up to the doorway. She didn't understand Vanja's reluctance to fight. He was as far from cowardice as it was possible to be. He resented her, though she couldn't understand why. If this worked, they would have the means to defeat Atramen utterly, even the Silence itself.

Cold metal was pressed into her hand. She grasped the Fragment and looked down at it. It... welcomed her. It felt right in her hands. The letters glittered. They were not yet shining like they had done when she had used the fragment before, but the shimmer that lay on them instead was a presage to the power that would soon blaze within her.

Over the constant music of the world around her, she could now hear, uppermost in her mind, the Great Song. It was irresistible. It was once glorious and bitter, joyful, and full of empty sadness. And it was incomplete. She could hear where the Song should continue and almost catch that part of the tune, but then it got lost and started from the beginning again. An endless cycle. She felt that if she listened hard and long enough, she could fathom the notes that would come next. She could even create new ones.

"Alecyn! No!" Mendel hissed at her. Alecyn realized she must have been speaking aloud.

She looked around her, blinking as though waking from sleep. How many of her thoughts had she given voice to?

"It is not for any ephemeral race to change the Great Song!" Mendel continued, lowering his head next to hers. "That is what the Great Silence tried to do, and it led to the breaking of the Song and the world!"

Alecyn shook her head, trying to clear it of the fog the Fragment had woven about her.

"I know. I wouldn't. The Fragment is what it is. The thing is alive. It puts its own thoughts in my head, Mendel. It seeks completion. Whether as part of the Great Song or a new Song. It doesn't matter. What is this thing, Mendel?"

She was looking at the Fragment in her hands with horror. It still whispered to her through the music, telling her of the power she could wield.

"It is part of... everything. Everything around us. Everything that has ever been or will ever be. It is trying to fit you into its world. You are the sorceress. It is helping you become that."

Alecyn shut her eyes and tried to suppress the refrain from the Great Song that kept repeating in her mind. "I do not want power. I want to heal. I will not be like the Silence. I will be the healer."

She repeated her mantra repeatedly, and the glorious symphony of the Great Song faded into the background, allowing the other music around her to make itself heard. The overwhelming thought left her with the impression that it willingly withdrew. Biding its time. "Can you force it to lie here?" Alecyn asked the struggling Kajani.

She winced at the noise from the Mute, though it was muffled through her earplugs. One of the Kajani was wrapping a leather cord across the middle of the head, forcing the faceplate to close. Alecyn sighed with relief when he pulled it tight. Alecyn thought the Kajani with the cord was female; she had smaller ears than the other two, without the pronounced tufts off the top that they had. Then, the three Kajani forced the creature down. Others offered stakes. They wrapped the rope around the stakes before forcing them into the cracks between the courtyard's flagstones.

Alecyn knelt beside the struggling figure and forced herself to examine it. It wore the familiar black carapace, swinging and sliding. The plates moved, causing black mucus to ooze and briefly exposing greyish flesh. Its head looked as though it wore a helmet fused to its shoulders, with no visible neck. It glistened wetly and kept straining open a finger's width before shutting with a snap. Amidst the symphony of the world, she sought its song. She found it discordant, painfully noisy, and chaotic. She allowed the song of the Mute to take center stage in her mind, the other music dimming into a buzz. Allowing it to wash over her, she looked for the fragments of human music.

"She listened for whatever was left of the creature's humanity that the creature might retain, even if they are diminished. "The creature will invariably maintain some aspects of the Song with which it was born, regardless of whether it is damaged or tainted." She didn't see who he was talking to but assumed the Kajani were watching. They had been hard to convince. Not helped by the single-minded opposition of Jerad and the Nelim to her plan. But she knew she could do it. She could heal a Mute and restore its lost humanity to it.

But she couldn't find it. Was this Mute too far gone? She opened her eyes, glaring at the captive creature.

"I can't hear it. I cannot believe it has gone so far that there is nothing left of what it was. It still has a human shape. It cannot have deviated that much!"

Mendel was kneeling beside her. Krissker was standing watch, but his ears were turning in all directions, and he kept looking up towards the gateway where Kajani and Nelim were fighting side by side. Alecyn closed her eyes again and concentrated. There was the obscene travesty of a Song. It was filthy and... wrong. Unnatural. But it was the twisted, mutated remnants of a natural Song. She believed there was something left in this Song if only she could get a feel for how the tune should go.

"There are other races that look like humans, are there not?" Mendel said diffidently. Alecyn opened her eyes wide in shock, her head whipping towards Mendel so fast that her hair flew around her face.

"Say that again!" she demanded breathlessly.

Mendel looked uncomfortable, as though he had done something wrong.

"You said it can't be so far gone. That it still has a human form. But this isn't just a human form, is it?"

That's when it clicked into place. "Mendel, you are a genius! How could I have been so deaf?!"

Now she could hear it. Just like reading a song's lyrics, the words suddenly jumped out in absolute clarity where they once had been indistinct. She couldn't hear the remnants of a human Song because this Mute had never been human. It was Kajani! She laughed aloud with relief. For one horrible moment, fear consumed her as she thought that all was lost. But now she knew what she needed to do. She focused her mind on the strange, savage, alien sounds of the Kajani song. She let it flow through her, following its difficulties, soaring themes, and rhythmic pulsing passages. Then she heard the Great Song emanating from the fragment. She allowed it to rise in volume in her mind. Alecyn began to sing.

There were no words. Her voice was its own instrument, and the music poured from it. She wove the melody of the Great Song with the broken, fragmented Song of the Kajani. Now that she knew what to listen for, she realized she could hear it all around her. She drew the power from her own spirit, infusing the music with it, giving it power. The broken fragments healed, and the discordant notes rang true. Where there had been breaks between strands of notes, now there was an entire tune.

Time was immaterial. The sensation was as fleeting as dust in the wind. There was only the music, the power flowing from her, and the Fragment.

She was dimly aware of Mendel's gasp and didn't need to look to know what was happening. The bound figure before her was sounding more like Kajani. She knew what Mendel and the others were seeing. The carapace was fading before their eyes, replaced by fur. The helmet was becoming a feline feature. The Mute was being healed.

"No!" Vanja bellowed.

Alecyn opened her eyes, still singing. Jerad was hurled out through the door of the keep. He missed the steps and landed in a heap at the bottom. Vanja hurtled out of the keep behind him, blades drawn. His warriors were with him. All had daubed dark streaks across their face, and Alecyn realized it was blood. They had weeping cuts on their arms and had smeared the dark blue blood in patterns across their faces.

Jerad was stumbling to his feet, a whip bow in his hand, which he lashed out at Vanja. The weapon wrapped itself around one bladed forelimb, and Vanja pulled it back effortlessly. But Jerad had expected this and was already running hard and using the momentum from Vanja's pull to increase his speed. He held a dagger in one hand, which he struck hilt first at the side of Vanja's head. The big Nelim blocked the blow, but Jerad kicked out hard at his knee, connecting and forcing Vanja to drop as his leg buckled.

Jerad leaped away from his slashing bladed limbs and recoiled his whip bow, reversing the dagger in his other hand to show the blade.

"What goes on here?!" roared Krissker, leaping to Jerad's side.

"Vanja is a traitor!" Jerad hissed. "He had his men jump me when I went inside."

Krissker growled deep in his throat, turning golden eyes on the Nelim. His black lips were pulled back to reveal the full extent of his teeth. Other Kajani gathered, lowering themselves to all fours, shoulders bunched with muscle. Their heads were low, their eyes intent, teeth bared.

"I will not stand by and let another mystic deprive me of my birthright!" Vanja snarled.

"Vanja! Can't you see what's happening? It's possible to heal mutes. We can turn the creatures of the Silence and bring them back to what they were. We can win the war!" Jerad said desperately.

"No!" Vanja was working himself up into a towering fury. "My destiny is battle. To fight and die against the Great Enemy! Erevar and his mystics denied me my birthright, and now this human is trying to do the same! I betrayed the Heart so my brothers and I could meet our destiny in battle. We will not be refused now.

Alecyn was aware of Mendel moving to stand before her where she knelt. She fought to keep her concentration, her Song wavering. One of Vanja's Nelim moved slightly, a flicker of one of its hind limbs. Something tugged at her temple, forcing her to turn her head slightly. There was no sensation of pain, just an odd pressure. Then she felt warmth spilling down her cheek, and something was spilling into her eyes. In shock, she stopped. Finding herself dropping to her knees. Lifting her hands to her head, they came away with bright red blood. The next few moments were a silent blur. Her world receded, framed in black. She saw Jerad lashing out with the whip bow as Kajani charged, howling into the Nelim ranks. Vanja came forward, one hind limb ending at the first joint where the bow had neatly severed it. Now, Vanja came forward to meet Jerad's single blade. Someone was pulling her back, Mendel. Something was being pressed to her head, and it would be to staunch the bleeding. She was bleeding from a head wound. Blackness. Battle. Blackness.

****

Alecyn was looking down at the castle. She saw Krissker's Kajani mowing down Vanja's Nelim in the courtyard. Jerad and Vanja remained locked in single combat amid the carnage. Mendel was dragging her unconscious body across the courtyard towards the walls. The figure staked out in the courtyard was becoming a Mute once again. She realized she could feel the rough stone beneath her, feel Mendel's hands under her arms, the pulsing pain in her head where the Nelim had struck her down. But she was ethereal, touching nothing around her. She rose higher and looked out beyond the walls. Nelim and Kajani formed a line around the castle gates, beyond which was a pile of Mute and human bodies. They fought as one, Kajani charging the enemy, Nelim riding them and striking with their long hind limbs. They pushed back the mass of attackers, and then the Kajani stood, Nelim leaping lightly to their feet. The Kajani then fought while the Nelim rested.

She could hear the collected Songs of humans somewhere in the south. It was out of sight, but she could hear their themes carried to her. If she concentrated, she could hear individuals distinguish between the inhabitants of what surely must be Fearnot, one by one. The world lurched around her, the landscape dashing by. She willed herself to a halt. Even a passing thought had been enough to send her spirit from racing to that place. She needed to be back in her body. She needed to be conscious and complete the healing she had been attempting. Then a thought occurred to her. It had been lurking in the back of her mind. Where was Atramen? Where were his sorcerers? From everything she had learned of him, he had minions with terrible magic. Why wasn't it used?

She rushed back over to the castle and hovered uncertainly. Her priority was to reenter her body, yet this presented an opportunity to uncover vital knowledge. She looked down. Vanja stood alone, dead Nelim around him, live Kajani stalking in a circle. Jerad stood before him.

His Song was a strident, raging torrent of sound. His fury pulsed stronger than Vanja's bloodlust, louder than the Mute's Noise. It was the thundering march of a pure, berserker rage. She moved back towards her body, but something held her where she was. Despite her efforts to move, she lacked sufficient knowledge of the Spirit Road to understand how. She had been acting on instinct but was now restrained.

"Jerad! No! We must stand together! Please!"

He couldn't hear her. Suddenly, Jerad was charging. His sword arm was a blur, his blade catching the light and shining. Vanja was driven back. Two of his hind limbs hung limp, and another severed. Jerad's Song degenerated into Noise, losing its form in the furious torrent of hate and rage. Then Vanja's long arm knocked Jerad's blade aside. For a heartbeat, Jerad stood, arms wide, body exposed. Vanja plunged his blade through Jerad's body. Alecyn screamed as she saw it emerge from his, covered in blood. She fought against the force that held her pinned, screaming for Jerad as Vanja raised his body high in triumph before the Kajani engulfed him. Then something tugged at Alecyn. The world flew beneath her. She screamed her grief as fields, forests, hills, and mountains spun and flashed by her. She was a rag doll, helpless in the clutches of whatever force held her. Then, she was still. The world around her was still.

She stood atop a stone pillar high in a mountain range. Mist hid the depths of the drop beneath her. Sorrowful cries rose from the shrouded depths—cries of torment and unendurable agony, throat-ripping screams. A figure sat upon a raised dais. He wore a metal mask crafted into a laughing face.

"We meet at last, True Voice." The voice was deep and mellifluous. "My name is Atramen."

CHAPTER 17:
ADEMAR

Lucas watched as the enemy forces pushed the desperate defenders of Fearnot further back. Smoke from the fire they had encouraged blackening the sky to the east, where it rose. And the south, where the wind carried it. It drifted across the hilltop of the Aviary, making Lucas and his aides cough and splutter. He had told Tobias to hold on to the last man, and that help was coming. He knew it was hopeless as he sent the same futile message in all directions under attack. Those men would not need his order to hold their ground. What they protected was too important. He stared at the map of the village he had sketched on the parchment on the table. They were being pushed back everywhere. The Silence was winning. Despair choked him, and he wished fervently for Jerad. Never had he wished to be a child again, to be free of this terrible responsibility.

He realized a group of Stonemen was coming up the hill. They carried the prone figure of a man on their shoulders, bound and gagged. Lucas walked to meet them and bade them put the man on his feet. The Shrieker, standing, was taller than Lucas. He looked emaciated, as though he had been fasting for months. Cheekbones were jutted above hollow cheeks. His eyes resembled sunken, skull-like caverns. His neck seemed unnaturally long, supporting a bald, bony head. Lucas stepped close to the man. A rank smell greeted him, the smell of festering meat. He met the yellow eyes that glittered at him from within sunken sockets.

"We are about to be overrun. I will ensure that your head gets removed before our lines break. Your only hope of staying alive is to help us. I don't know why you haven't used magic against us. Song knows you could have conquered us months ago. I don't care. Use your magic to destroy the forces attacking us. I will kill you if you do not. Once we are safe, I will release you.

Lucas hoped he appeared steadfast and threatening. He felt like a little boy threatening an adult. There was no expression on the Shrieker's face. There was nothing to show if he was taking Lucas seriously. Then he nodded. There was a single movement. He resumed his silent stare. Lucas fought to keep surprise from his face and voice. He had to maintain an appearance of control as if he completely expected this. That was Jerad's way.

"Good. I am going to remove your gag now. That will be the only bond we remove. For now." He turned to the Stonemen. "Put your blades to his throat close enough to draw blood."

Suddenly, a ring of spear blades encircled the Shrieker's throat except where Lucas stood before him. The blades pressed in and produced beads of blood that trickled along the blades to the ground.

"Act against us, and you will be dead in a heartbeat. You may kill me and these men. But not, I think, all of them. Not in time to save yourself."

Lucas reached up and untied the gag, pulling it away from the man's mouth and forcing himself not to take steps back. The Shrieker worked his mouth restoring circulation lost because of his bonds.

"Thank you," he said. His voice was oddly accented and deep. "My lips were numb after so long." He was curiously soft-spoken.

"Will you help us?"

"For my life. Yes, I will. As I told those other men whom you threw in jail."

"You put a spell on them," Lucas said flatly.

Ademar smiled. "Guilty, I am afraid. I thought they might be of use. But then they never put a ring of steel around my throat."

He seemed at ease, only the unnatural rigidity of his head and neck suggesting any awareness of the blades poised to sever his head.

"Destroy the armies you sent to destroy us."

"First, they are not my armies at all. They belong to Atramen. Second, I would love to rain destruction down on them like you can't imagine…"

"But?"

"But. Was there a but? Yes, of course, there was a but. But... I think it's only fair to warn you of what will happen to all of us if I deploy magic. Here."

Lucas refused to look away from Ademar's gaze. Around him, he knew Stonemen were holding their spears white-knuckled and holding their courage even tighter. All it would take was one of them becoming spooked, and Fearnot's only hope could die with blood gushing from a severed artery. Smoke drifted around them, temporarily isolating Lucas and Ademar from the other men.

"What will happen?" Lucas asked.

"The Black Hand will…" He paused as though choosing his words. "Pulverize your city."

Lucas felt the situation spinning further from his control. Too many new factors to consider. He could not decide this fast.

"Who or what is the Black Hand?"

"The right hand of the Great Silence himself. The position Atramen held until he made his bid for supremacy and ended up locked up in Argent behind his Veil. She attacked Atramen not long after we entered the Southlands. Then she started hunting us down. One by one. She would do frightful things to those she caught. That's why I let you catch me."

"That's why there is no magic," Lucas murmured.

"Quiet," said Ademar, as though someone had directed the statement to him. "We had to remain quiet, acting as generals but unable to use our Noise for fear of bringing the Black Hand down on us. She is powerful. And quite ruthless."

"So, what do you want?" Lucas demanded. The wind shifted, and he could see the hillside again. A runner was dashing up the hill from the south. A rider was approaching from the east. He held up his hands towards both and turned back to Ademar.

"One of your gigantic birds to escape. I will strike at the forces encircling you and do as much damage as possible before fleeing. I can give you a fighting chance."

"No."

"Then we will all die. The Mutes will not pass up the chance to slaughter a helpless Shrieker. We made them. Some remember that even if they don't remember their former existence. They remember the pain, though." He smiled for the first time as though the word pleased him. Or it was a memory evoked by his words. A memory of inflicting pain. Lucas felt sick.

"No," he said, fixing the gag back into Ademar's mouth. "Hold him." He ordered the Stonemen. Ademar's eyes followed him as he stepped away.

"General Haverford." gasped the boy who had brought him Tobias' message earlier. "Master Tobias has fallen. The South has fallen. Mutes are in the city. They are spreading everywhere!"

The rider stood by impatiently. "General, sir." Lucas absently realized he knew the boy. It was the blacksmith's son. But what was his name? He found he couldn't remember. Fatigue lay on him heavily as he waited for fresh news of the disaster. All the time, he could feel Ademar's eyes boring into him.

"The fire is holding them, sir. Master Hanven says to tell you he can spare men to hold the south."

"No. Send them to the Great Hall. Instruct Master Hanven to bring everyone back to the Great Hall to avoid being attacked from the rear." He lost everything, and even if he played his one trump card... he would still lose everything. Unless he was lying. But there was no way to put that to the test. Lucas turned, suddenly resolute, unless he used the enemy's weapons against him.

"I need a blade." He said and had the satisfaction of seeing a frown skip across Ademar's brow.

A Stoneman slapped a short sword into Lucas' hand. He hefted the weapon as he advanced.

"I need one of you to hold a blade to his throat. The rest need to go to the Great Hall. Master Hanven will take command." Hanven was a good man, a farmer from the east country who had proved an excellent leader.

"I will stay with you, sir." Lucas' eyes flicked to the Stoneman who had spoken. It was Master Lother, one of Fearnot's farriers. He was old enough to be Lucas' grandfather but was as tough as oak and still as strong as an ox. Lucas had never known him to show deference to any man, even Jerad. As the others ran down the hill to their new position, they removed the blades.

"Now," said Lucas with a smile. "I don't believe you. So, we are going to try again. And every time I hear a lie in your voice. I am going to remove a piece of you."

He snatched the gag from Ademar's mouth, and Lother pressed his blade so tight that Ademar's voice came out as a strangled hiss.

"I am telling you the truth! She will kill us all!"

"Lie," Lucas said. He knew the Shriekers loved to inflict pain. It was the source of their power. He intended to become one of them. He slowly pushed his blade against Ademar's side, slicing through his robes and into the flesh beneath. The blade sank deeper and easier than Lucas expected, as though the tissue was already soft with decay. He twisted his wrist and then pulled down, slicing off a chunk of meat from Ademar's ribs. The man screamed. He threw back his head, and the movement caused Lother's blade to dig deeper into his throat.

"Try again, Ademar."

"She would kill me if she could find me."

"That has the ring of truth. Can she find you?"

"Yes..."

"Lie," Lucas said flatly. This time, he scythed the blade down the outside of Ademar's right leg, slicing away his bonds and carving out a chunk of flesh just above the knee. Blood spattered the grass. Ademar screamed again, full-throated.

"It is not a lie! It is not a lie! She could find me, given time!"

"Better." Lucas held his short sword up, so the point rested on Ademar's cheek. "Tell me more."

Lother was smiling wolfishly. Lucas felt sick. There was a perverse thrill running through him. To inflict pain like this on one who would have done much worse to the people of Fearnot. A man who had given his soul to evil. Part of him enjoyed seeing the pain and fear in the Shrieker's eyes. Another part wanted to run. Far away and not stop.

"Lucas?" Adellin's voice came out of the smoke falteringly.

"Get away from here, Adellin!" Lucas yelled.

"What are you doing? Why aren't you at the Great Hall... I…"

Lucas hardened himself. Ademar was about to crack. They couldn't allow him a reprieve now. He pressed the blade in until the point drew blood from the eyelid, making Ademar's eye bulge outwards. The Shrieker gabbled.

"Please! Please, don't! I will tell you the truth! I will do as you ask! Please, not my eyes!"

"Lucas!" The smoke shifted again, and Adellin could see Lucas clearly.

She saw the blood that covered him and Ademar. Saw Lucas' grim smile as his prisoner begged. She rushed towards him. "Lucas! No! Not like this! You are not like them!"

She grabbed his arm, but Lucas threw her off with a snarl. Didn't she understand he had to become like them to beat them? The issue of terror required appropriate measures to be taken. If they were prepared to inflict pain, he had to be prepared to inflict greater. Adellin landed on her backside, immediately got to her feet, and rushed back to Lucas. This time, he threw her down with a backhand swipe that caught her across the face. She hit the ground with a gasp and, for a moment, lay staring at him, one hand to the side of her face.

"Get away from me!" Lucas snarled. He turned back to Ademar. "One. Last. Chance!" He screamed, spittle flying from his mouth.

"She will sense my power. But it will take her time to find me in the Spirit Realm. But she will. She will follow the scent of my power, even if I don't use it again. She will find me eventually. Your only hope is to run.

"My only hope is to find Atramen. If she hasn't already killed him". Ademar replied.

Lucas stepped back, releasing the pressure on Ademar's eye. "Do it. And when you finish it, I will release you. You have my word."

He dropped the blade and indicated that Lother drop his. The farrier seemed reluctant, with a look of disappointment on his face. Lucas felt revulsion for the man's obvious enjoyment of Ademar's pain, then berated himself as no different. It didn't matter that he did it to save Fearnot. He was like them. A torturer. A killer. He couldn't look at Adellin. The anger that had boiled in him when she had tried to interfere was subsiding, but it had overwhelmed him for a moment. She was better off without him.

Stepping behind Ademar, Lucas loosened his bonds.

"Do it." He ordered.

Ademar nodded and drew a breath. He began to sing.

****

Lucas didn't know how long the music lasted. The screams of the Mutes lasted longer. Later, reports told him they had stopped where they stood. The terrible music had rolled out from the hilltop, the sound of pure agony, distilled suffering. Lucas wanted to vomit, watching such sounds pouring from another human being. No, he wasn't human. Not any longer. This creature in front of him was a devil in human form. He had lost any right to be called human. But he had kept his bargain. The Shrieker's magic had laid waste to the Mutes where they stood and in the worst pain imaginable. Lucas didn't want to know what Ademar had done to them. It was done.

Ademar watched him warily as he summoned a stormbird down into the Aviary pen. Lucas beckoned Ademar to follow him and walked towards the giant bird.

"There are a few things you need to know about riding a stormbird…"

He began. "First, you see up there above its head?" He pointed, and as Ademar turned his full attention to the bird, Lucas coolly sidestepped and slashed his sword across the man's throat. Ademar's eyes widened as his head fell back, and his throat yawned wide. His mouth opened, but before he could utter a sound, Lucas slammed the sword down into the wound he had caused, beheading him. Like a puppet whose strings had been cut, the body of the former Shrieker slumped to the ground.

Lucas stood over him.

"I never said how I would release you, Ademar." He breathed and walked away.

CHAPTER 18:
THE ALIEN WITHIN

Alecyn found she had backed away to the very edge of the pillar she stood on. She looked behind and down, but the mist had obscured the chasm. However, enough was revealed that she knew about the fall that awaited her. Vertigo dizzied her, and she hastily stepped forward. She clenched her fists and resolved not to look about her to the edges of her impossible perch. It was small, far too small to be standing so high and rigid. She could cover the top of the pillar in half a dozen long strides and yet seemed to stand on something solid and unyielding. She felt it should have been swaying precariously under its top-heavy weight.

But the alternative was no better. Looking straight ahead, she had to confront the masked figure that sat before her.

"I have been searching for you, True Voice. Ever since I felt the barrier between your world and mine weakening once more. You know you are not the first of your kind to come here?"

"Yes. I have met Rose." Alecyn replied and was proud of herself that her voice didn't shake.

"There will be others, I'm sure. Onyx has not relented in his ambitions to alter the Great Song to his design. And the very fabric of reality thins with each manipulation. That is why it is so important that we work together."

"Why on earth would I help you?"

"Because, alone, neither of us is strong enough to withstand Onyx. Even with our respective fragments." Suddenly, there was a slab of gleaming gold nestled in the crook of his arm. He stroked gloved fingers over it, and an intoxicating melody sprang into the air. It enveloped her, soothing her.

"He has a fragment of his own and will attempt to gain the last piece from the humans. With two, he will be unassailable. Do you want this world ripped apart, your own with it and countless others besides?"

The tune continued as Atramen's fingers danced over the complex inscriptions covering his fragment. Her head felt heavy, and part of her questioned whether any enemy of the Great Silence could really be an enemy of hers. Didn't it make sense to join with him, to learn from him and together…

"Alecyn!" The voice was like breaking glass. It crashed through the spell Atramen was weaving about her. Alecyn jumped, realizing she had been slumping to the ground, one hand and one knee touching the rock. She staggered to her feet. The voice was familiar. The voice had been Eevee's!

"This place is not real! You are back in the dreamlands. Here you are as strong as he!" Alecyn saw a ghostly shape standing between herself and Atramen. It was a cat, a shape she knew so well. She reached out toward Eevee, but Atramen was on his feet. A roar came from him, a sound of fury and violence, and the shape dispersed like dust on the wind. Atramen strode towards her purposefully. But Alecyn knew what Eevee had been talking about. She had behaved as though this was the physical world, and its immutable nature bound her. It was not the physical realm; it was the Spirit Road. It was like the Heart. Here she could decide what was real just as much as Atramen could. She watched him approach, a gloved hand reaching for her, and then the rock crumbled beneath his feet.

Atramen had time for one startled look downwards and fell to land with a thump in soft grass. They were in a forest clearing. Butterflies danced in sunbeams that fell through the trees; the air was thick with the scent of wildflowers and sap. Alecyn drew a deep breath, wriggling her bare toes against the lush grass. Her flute was in her hand. Atramen looked up at her, and for a second, he froze. His still, golden face laughed, but his body spoke of shock. Then, with a growl, he was on his feet. The world flickered, the mountaintop returned, the forest grove returned, and the mountaintop peeked through the trees and vanished again.

"Stop this!" Atramen shouted as he sat on a deck chair on the porch of Alecyn's home on Earth. Alecyn sat on the porch rail, Eevee curled in her lap. She was as surprised as Atramen by this change. The scene hung about them both, tantalizing, and then was gone. She wanted to cry. Seeing her home brought on a wave of crippling homesickness. Atramen was staggering back from her as their surroundings whirled and changed dizzily.

"You are lighting us up like a beacon fire! She will come for both of us, you fool!" Atramen screamed, battering Alecyn. She looked at him, homesickness dying away and leaving an icy determination.

"I have decided that I will no longer tolerate being manipulated, Atramen. I set my path."

They were standing on the edge of a forest. A path of hard-packed, worn earth marked the edge of the trees, and beyond it, the land fell away as though cleaved by an axe. Stone walls and tall towers rose in the distance, separated from them by a steep gulf. Alecyn had been here before.

Here, overlooked by the dreaded Tall Towers, where she had first met Jerad. Jerad, who had died in his quest to see her safe. Jerad, who even now was breathing his last without her. Because this creature had pulled her from him, to let him die alone to play his pathetic power games. The anger was stoking hotter in Alecyn. The flute was gone, as were her clothes. In their place, a suit of shining armor worked with inscriptions and runes.

Atramen was backing away from her slowly. "You know this place in the real world?"

"I have stood on this very spot. And defeated the Black Hand. Twice." Alecyn replied grimly, and her voice rang with music. Music rumbled like thunder, shaking the trees and causing the ground to tremble.

"Great sorcerer, can you claim as much? You, who hid yourself in your stolen city? Atramen, the coward!" Atramen was flinching as though physically struck.

"You don't know what you're doing! You must listen to me!"

"No, I have listened enough. Your war ends here. You came looking for me, and you have found me. If you meet me in the real world, I will strip the flesh from your bones, you animal!" Alecyn was screaming at him now. Her armor was incandescent, the grass beneath her feet bursting into flames.

She stepped towards Atramen, leaving blackened, charred footsteps behind her. It was so easy. She could feel the fabric of this plane of reality as though it was clay beneath her fingers. She could twist it and mold it. She could tear it and destroy it. The armor she wore became part of her.

She could no longer tell where it ended and where her flesh began. A helm had appeared on her head and was now stretching to cover her face. It felt good. It felt right!

Atramen attacked desperately. A song arose from his throat, and power flared in him. Alecyn's overpowering harmony silenced the song completely. She couldn't consciously say how she was doing this. It felt as though something within her had awakened. It awakened into a world that perfectly suited it. And now it was stretching itself, bringing itself to the forefront of her mind, wielding her will like a sword. A sudden panicked terror rose within her, but she quickly snuffed it out. A strange song was riding the wind. It was unlike anything she had ever heard, and she knew it came from her.

Atramen howled and shrieked, and Noise was all he had left. Every attempt at Music had been batted away by the thing worn by Alecyn's form. It swirled about her like a cloud of angry wasps. A cloud of angry wasps whose buzzing faded and died beneath the Song of Alecyn's new form.

Strange thoughts were coursing through her. She felt contempt for this insignificant insect who thought himself so powerful but understood nothing of the force he wielded. She felt that the world was wrong. Someone had changed it. She knew how to make it right, how to make it suit her.

Without conscious thought, she directed the glorious symphony that was her Song toward the cowering, masked man. His mask fell away, cracked, and crumbled as he clutched it. Underneath, his skin was grey and scabbed. Lesions ravaged the remaining features of his face. There was no nose, and one eye was a scarred, empty socket. He reached up his gloved hand, and the leather turned to dust and blew away on the wings of Alecyn's great Song. He wailed at the sight of his ravaged flesh, beginning to curl in on himself.

"You are nothing," Alecyn told him. The helm completely covered her face now. She looked out through a layer of clear, crystalline material. "You were never meant to rule this world, and you will not have the Great Song."

Atramen had buried his face in the ground, covering his head with both arms.

"You can't be here!" He whispered. "You cannot be one of them!"

"I am. This world was ours, and it will be again. Your time is over, human."

"No, no, no, no!" Atramen wailed.

"Tell Rose," Alecyn said. She had realized the observer who watched her from a distance. The Black Hand had thought she was disguised and an adept of this plan. But she was a child learning to find its feet. The thing that had awakened inside Alecyn was born of this plain. The constraints of a physical form had never shackled it. Alecyn turned her head. The Black Hand took shape as a raven, darting and bobbing amid the chasm. "Atramen is done, and his fragment will be mine. I will burn down Kragen Onyx and take back my world."

The raven disappeared with a single cry. My world. My world. This is not my world. This is not my home. Alecyn felt as though she was being separated from her own body. A pressure was at work on her mind, imposing its thoughts on her. This is my world. Humans have warped it, but I have the power to... No! This was not her world! This was not her home! But the thing that had seized control had not just altered her body. It was altering her mind. She tried to recall Lake Wales, the view from her bedroom window, the summer evenings with Eevee at her feet, playing her flute. She tried to recall Jerad. To bring back to her mind the grief and loss she had felt when she saw his body struck down.

But it became muted, growing pale and indistinct. Alien thoughts and memories were intruding. What was happening to her? Atramen was gone.

While she was distracted, Atramen had left the Spirit Road and entered the physical world. Alecyn raised her hands in front of her face. Her flesh was gone. The armor was a glassy substance alive with crawling lights, but within which there was no sign of her arm. What was she becoming? She was returning to herself. To her true self.

"No! This is not me!" Alecyn shrieked. The effort to force those words out through the crystal shell that encased her felt like she was tearing off her own skin. "I am Alecyn Johnsenn of Lake Wales, Florida! I. Am. Human!"

She hurled herself off the cliff.

CHAPTER 19:
THE GREAT ONE

Alecyn woke with a scream. Mendel leaped back from her, startled. All she could do for a moment was stare at the sky, breathing hard. She was breathing. She could feel the air drawn past her lips, down her throat. Her hands were cold against stone, fingers clawed at the unyielding surface, nails catching on the uneven flagstones. There was no armor, no crystal shell absorbing her flesh and bone. She was human again. And this was the physical world. Jerad!

She sat up, ignoring the sharp pain in her head. Mendel was trying to hold her down, saying something about bleeding, about a head injury, but she pushed him away. Around them lay dead Nelim and a couple of dead Kajani. Two Nelim held Vanja fast. His bladed hind limbs were severed. Head hung, body limp. Krissker stood before him, the body of Jerad lying on the ground at his feet. Krissker held a paw high above Vanja's head, claws extended.

"Stop!" Alecyn shouted, and she poured every ounce of willpower she could muster into her cry. The word reverberated around the keep, causing giant, bloody Kajani warriors to shrink back, baring their teeth in fright. Krissker looked around, his arm falling. Alecyn climbed to her feet, knocking away a supporting arm from Mendel. The pain and dizziness she could feel were immaterial. She was human. Her body was fully human. She felt sick and didn't know whether it was the head wound she had suffered or the memory of that change that had come over her on the Spirit Road.

"No more deaths! Not Nelim or Kajani or Mutes. None!" The killing and suffering had gone on long enough. The key to ending the war and rendering Atramen helpless lay before her. She would use her power to heal, and it would stop the killing at a stroke. She felt a chill like a cold, inhuman thought skittered across her consciousness. Better they all die.

"No!"

A shockwave raced out from Alecyn, knocking anyone standing to the ground. The ropes holding the Mute staked out in the ground snapped. It scrabbled towards the gates, its inhuman form fully restored.

"Stay!" Commanded Alecyn. With a cry of pain, Mendel dropped the song fragment he had picked up from the ground when Alecyn stood. It was shining bright and burning hot. Alecyn didn't need to touch it to use its power. There was a connection between them. Something had changed in her when she was on Spirit Road. A part of her she had never known existed was awake. But she was still human! The thought was resolute. She would not become whatever had taken over. That alien thing that desired nothing less than to wipe the world clean of life and start again.

The Mute stopped as though frozen in time. It didn't move. It was so easy now. Her will directed her Voice, and her Voice changed the world around her to suit her needs. The Song fragment was crooning to her, forming part of the background symphony she could hear. She was drawing in that flow of otherworldly power and mingling it with her own inner music. It was all done with no more conscious thought than breathing.

The power was hers. She desperately listened to the surrounding music while searching for a theme. Dismissed the Nelim and Kajani songs, the warped human song of the Mute. She listened for that rousing anthem that was the soul of her hero, Jerad. It was gone. There was no trace left that she could hear. Even using the immense power of the Fragment. Despair filled her. It gouged out something from within her, leaving an emptiness that was terrifying in its totality. She stumbled to Jerad's prone form, falling to her knees. Around her, all was still. The Kajani watched her from feral crouches. Vanja stared open-mouthed. Mendel's eyes were wide. She stared at the man who had risked so much to find her. What had made him so determined to risk his life to save a stranger? He was handsome. So handsome. Bravery marked his actions and honor. And his sadness made Alecyn want to hold him in her arms, pulling his head to her chest. And now he was gone.

"No! This will not happen! I will not lose him! Do you hear me?!" She shouted but didn't know who she was shouting at. She felt like she might explode if she didn't let it out. A sickening feeling was tearing through her. A loss so great it threatened to drive away any conscious thought. It was unbearable, and she did everything she could to stop it. There was so much power around her. Deep in the earth, in the souls of the beings who shared the keep with her. In the misshapen, corrupted souls of the creatures who strove to enter the keep and who lurked in the trees beyond. And she knew how to use it. With all that power at her command, nothing was beyond her. She drew on it.

She sang the Song of Jerad. The tune she knew by heart, the melody that was his. Without words, she sang and infused that song with all the power she could. Jerad's Song rang out from within the battered, moss-covered walls of the keep. It soared above the walls and rode the wind. Her body reverberated with it, and it was glorious. She reached out and took Jerad's hand. Stopped singing because she had felt the Song wrap itself around his dead form. She could feel it taking on a life of its own. The terrible wound in his chest was gone. Jerad opened his eyes.

The first thing he saw was her. She held his hand, the other resting on his head. She knew she was smiling, and tears were flooding from her eyes. His Song was free of her now, and it didn't need the power she had given it or her own Voice to give it life. It was part of him again, stronger than before, whole. There were gasps from around the keep. Kajani fell to their knees in awe. Jerad sat up slowly, running a wandering hand across his torn shirt.

"I remember fighting Vanja. I remember dying." He still hadn't looked away from Alecyn. She didn't think she had seen anything as beautiful as his eyes. How could she have ever chosen to return home over him?

There was no doubt in her mind now. She wanted to be wherever he was.

"I... I brought you back, Jerad." His name was tentative in her mouth as though unfamiliar. She felt like she was discovering it anew, saying it for the first time since she had acknowledged to herself how she felt. "I healed you."

He kissed her. It was a sudden movement, one hand cupping her face at once tenderly and firmly. And Alecyn forgot everything. They lost all sense of time, where they were, and what was happening. There was no sensation but his hands on her skin and his lips on hers. When he pulled back, he was breathing hard, as was she. He stammered, trying to speak but seeming just as deprived of the ability as she felt.

"Great One." came Krissker's voice.

Alecyn finally looked away from Jerad. Krissker was on his knees, hands flat on the ground. "Great One, you have done the impossible. You have the power over death itself. My warriors and I are yours, body, and soul." He drew a single claw across his forearm, cutting deep through fur and skin to draw blood. Alecyn realized that all of them were doing it. They allowed their blood to drip to the ground and then carefully licked at the wound.

"I accept your oaths, Krissker. I hope to prove myself worthy of your loyalty." She hoped it was the right thing to say. Krissker and the others seemed satisfied with her words. One look at Jerad's face told her she had done the right thing in his eyes. She tore her gaze away, conscious that she couldn't just sit staring at him. Remembering the Mute, she was about to stand when a sudden wave of dizziness swept over her.

"Help me. But make sure it's not obvious. He contrived to help her to her feet while making it look like he embraced her. She leaned slightly on his shoulder as she looked for the Mute. It still stood frozen in place, but now she realized the sheer effort she was exerting to hold it there. She had divided her concentration without thinking about it, but fatigue ate away at her, and she realized how much she was attempting. Mendel, ever watchful, had seen the weakness and was by her side. He carried the Fragment, and his face was as pale as she had ever seen it.

"You must not draw too much of yourself, Alecyn." He whispered. "I did not know one person could hold so much power to do what you have done, but…"

"I don't," Alecyn replied as she walked towards the Mute. Her legs felt rubbery, like they might collapse under her at any moment, but she reached it. Mendel followed her, head close to hers. "I drew my power from the world and all of you." She finished. "I still am."

Mendel jerked back as though stung. "You must not! That is a thing of great evil! You must stop!"

"No!" Alecyn said aloud. The Kajani stirred. They were on their feet and ready to leap to her defense. "I will do whatever it takes to end this war. Whatever I must."

Mendel was shaking his head, backing away from her. "No. This is not the way Alecyn. Please. It will change you."

Jerad looked from one to the other in confusion. "What is he saying, Alecyn?"

"He doesn't understand magic. Not really. Not like me. I am the True Voice, remember?" Alecyn replied. She glared at Mendel. "And there is one more thing I must do. You remember what we were about before Vanja…"

"Yes," said Jerad shortly. He looked at Vanja, who was still crouched on the ground, his head twitching from place to place. The bodies of the warriors who had followed him lay strewn about him. A Kajani growled.

"Enough! No more killing. I will hear why Vanja betrayed us and his own people. But there will be no more killing! Do you understand?" She demanded of all. She looked Jerad in the eye. "Even you, Jerad."

He looked at her for a long moment, and once again, she felt the butterflies in her stomach. Then he put a hand to his heart. "By my Song, Great One. I swear."

Alecyn turned back to the Mute. Now that she knew what to look for, its broken travesty of a song was clear to her. Ignoring the increasing shakiness, she drew more power and began to Sing.

CHAPTER 20:
IN DREAMS

Power coursed through her. How could this be wrong? It was glorious. As she embraced the energy that was every living thing around her, she felt a harmony that she had never experienced before. The lives of her companions nestled, bright and gemlike, in the palm of her hands. Beyond them was the wider world, the immensity of nature. It was an ocean of life, and she was drinking it in. And through her, she wove that energy into a Song more beautiful than anything she had ever heard. It felt like she was listening to music for the first time. Her heart rang with it like a tolled bell. She ironed out dissonances in the melody and erased discordant notes. Under her touch, the Song was pure and whole, fitting into the world around it as she knew it must do.

Alecyn wasn't aware of the gasps of those around her. She couldn't see the Kajani prostrating on the ground. Couldn't see the tears in Mendel's eyes as his head slowly shook before he turned away violently, stumbling towards the gate before falling to his knees. She didn't feel Jerad's hand on her shoulder or hear his voice. The Song was everything. It was complex, like intricate weaving. And she followed every musical thread to its conclusion. Nowhere could she allow corruption to linger. The sun wheeled in the sky, and her body screamed for release as she knelt before the prostrate form that had once been a Mute. No longer.

The body of a young Kajani female now lay on the stone of the courtyard. She had long, dark fur and a wide, oval face. Alecyn was dimly aware of this as she felt her face touching the stones. Jerad was casting a cloak over the Kajani. She was naked, and her chest was rising and falling in the movements of a deep sleep. Sleep. That sounded good. No, she needed to do something first. She forced herself to her feet. The sun was directly overhead, bright, and warm. She felt a deep chill, though, and shivered uncontrollably. She had to use both hands to push herself up into an upright position.

"You did it!" Jerad spoke with a tone of admiration. "You brought her back."

"Surely, nothing can be beyond you, Great One," Krissker purred.

Alecyn felt the pulse of the sleeping Kajani, pressed her head to the female's chest, and listened to her breathing. She pulled back the cloak, checking her body for any sign of abnormalities or any remnant of the monster she had been. There was nothing. She was perfect. Alecyn wondered if she had restored the Kajani to the form she had possessed before she fell into Atramen's hands or something better. She had been striving for perfection.

Had she restored the female instead to a Kajani ideal? It seemed irrelevant, though a small voice in her mind warned her it wasn't.

She sat back, except it was more like a collapse. She thudded back into a sitting position, swaying further until Jerad's arms surrounded her.

"Enough. You have done enough for one day, girl." He was picking her up.

She laughed at his choice of words. Didn't he know she was the True Voice? Girl indeed!

"You need to get some sleep and recover your strength. Mendel, I need you to watch over her. Mendel!"

She was being placed on something soft and pungent. She realized it was a Kajani. Massive arms enfolded her, the fur impossibly soft and warm.

Sleep washed over her, and she snuggled into the feline embrace. A deep voice rumbled.

"Leave her to me, human. Safe as in her mother's arms."

She opened her eyes briefly. The Kajani against whom she so comfortably snuggled was auburn with flashes of black, the voice was female. Alecyn didn't know which Kajani it was, but it didn't matter. Her thick fur was the perfect eiderdown.

"I will be okay. I need to shut my eyes... just for a few minutes." Alecyn closed her eyes. She felt a human hand on her forehead.

"Take as long as you need. Sleep. You have earned it. Perseffa will take care of you."

Alecyn opened her eyes once more to look up at Jerad. Behind him was Mendel, sitting against the wall and clutching his knees to his chest. The Nelim watched her with hooded eyes and a blank face. She tried to smile at him, tried to say something. But the effort was too great. She slept.

****

She woke to darkness except for the flickering of a campfire. She stretched languidly, remaining within the embrace of her Kajani protector.

She felt wonderfully refreshed.

"Thank you for looking after me, Perseffa," she said, dimly remembering the name. There was no reply. She looked back over her shoulder and saw the gaping throat of the dead Kajani. Alecyn screamed, pushing herself back. It was only then that she realized Perseffa's blood had drenched her. It covered her back, arms, and legs. Her hair was sticky and matted with it. She scrambled to her feet, stumbling away. The golden-haired Kajani rolled onto her back from the impetus of Alecyn pushing against the body.

Someone had ripped open her throat. Alecyn's heels kicked against something soft. Looking down, she saw Mendel's slumped body. Someone had decapitated him. Full wakefulness hit her like a slap in the face. She looked around the shadowy, fire-lit room. Bodies lay everywhere. Flies misted the air. An acrid coppery tang was thick in her nostrils.

"Jerad!" Alecyn shouted. "Jerad, where are you?"

"Alecyn!" She heard his voice and turned to the doorway. It was black, and nothing was visible from the night before. Then Jerad was there. His face was pale, sword in hand. She moved towards him but stopped as a black shape erupted from his chest. His mouth opened wide, but no sound came from it. A dark figure appeared behind him, featureless, a shadow of deeper black against the night. Someone clamped their hand to the top of his head and brutally withdrew the blade that had pierced him. Jerad's lifeless body was flung aside to crunch limply against the stone. Rose stepped into the room.

She wore dark, glistening armor that hugged her body like a second skin. The same smooth material encased her head, except for her face. Her lips were glossy red, as though she wore lipstick.

Her right arm ended in a black blade which dripped with Jerad's blood. Its surface rippled and flowed, becoming an armored hand.

"Sorry for the mess, babes," Rose said. "But it was the only way to get a word with you alone. Those cats just weren't keen on me speaking to you. Can you imagine? Trying to keep us apart, the only two true humans in this entire world."

"What have you done?" Alecyn said in horror, her eyes never leaving Jerad's crumpled form.

Suddenly, a wind was tearing through the keep, driving her backward.

The stones tore themselves free of their ancient mortar to fly into the air, sucked into a tightening whirlwind. The entire castle and world were being torn apart. It was coming apart and flying up into the vortex above.

"Oh, don't mind that. I was always dramatic. What's the point of power if you can't do something truly spectacular?" Rose said, airing her hand at the chaos that now surrounded them.

"I'm dreaming," Alecyn said. Her heart was racing. Fear filled her. But there was a kernel of calm within. She knew she had the power to destroy the Black Hand. Not the Hand's skill or experience, though.

"Of course you are, darling." Rose laughed. "Slow today, aren't you? Do you think I would dare go head-to-head with you after what you have done? Take on a fragment bearer? I may be psychotic, sweetie, but I am not stupid."

Alecyn forced herself to stillness, ignoring the winds that plucked at her, threatening to lift her off her feet. It was an illusion. Once again, it was the Spirit Road, and this woman's whirlwind was just a pretense to disturb and frighten her. Alecyn began humming a comforting tune of her childhood, cloaking herself in the reassuring melody, letting the music strengthen her. She picked up her flute. She wore a t-shirt with the inscription from the fragment here, but not in the real world.

The wind slowed. As the haze of whirling debris settled, Alecyn conjured a peaceful, sunlit glade. The grass was deep and sweet-scented, wildflowers in a profusion of colors accented the shades of green. It was a grove she had come across in the Heart what seemed like a lifetime ago. Rose was shaking her head.

"This will not do. I am a city girl. Besides, there is someone who wants a word with you."

Alecyn felt her control shifting, the forest glade shimmering and fading into darkness. As she had done with Atramen, she concentrated on restoring her control. But this time, the force working against her was immeasurably more powerful. Control was being taken from her, slowly but surely.

"What do you want?" Alecyn snarled. "Does Atramen want a rematch?

Rose's laughter peeled about Alecyn. "Atramen? A pathetic excuse for a man. He knew his time was up when the Master pulled me from the Gateway. I have been stalking his Shriekers, hunting them down for sport here and in the waking world. Without them, he is nothing. Between us, honey, we will cut Atramen down to size. You destroy his army, and I destroy his sorcerers."

Alecyn was confused. Her control slipped further. The forest disappeared to be replaced with shifting shadows and a chill breeze. She felt an unyielding, damp stone beneath her feet.

"I don't understand. Atramen follows the Silence..."

"He was Kragen Onyx's right hand. Until I came along. Now he is a renegade. But he is not the reason I am here. My master wants to speak to you. Kragen Onyx has commanded your presence."

Rose's voice quivered with fear and awe as she spoke the name. "But why should I take you before him? He is far from here, and he is not omnipotent. Why should I let you take what was supposed to be mine?" Suddenly, anger flared in the woman's voice. Her face twisted with hate.

Alecyn realized she was dangerously unstable, her personality flickering into a psychotic rage at the drop of a hat. But had she always been this way? Or was this what Kragen Onyx had done to her? Rose was looking at her now from beneath lowered brows, and her face was still. Her black, impenetrable eyes were unmoving, and shapes shifted across her skin like smoke. They were dark and flowing. There was a hint of white between her lips as they parted in a silent snarl.

"I will not join him. No matter what he offers me."

"You have no idea." Rose hissed, advancing towards Alecyn. Alecyn backed away. The chilly mist was clearing. They were standing amid ancient stone columns, each pitted and flaking. Beneath their feet were the remains of stone, now erupting with trees and plants. It was a ruin. Rose laughed. It was a harsh sound, jarring. Alecyn recognized the power of Noise being directed at her. It shook rivulets of dust from the pillars. Alecyn brought her flute to her mouth without conscious thought, and her darting, dancing melody met the destructive Noise and countered it.

Alecyn changed their surroundings. She did not stop playing but somehow split her concentration between the tune she wove against Rose and changing the dreamscape of the Spirit Road. They stood beside a lake. In the distance was the warm glow of electric lights. A full moon rippled on the mirrored surface of the water. Silent parkland, framed by manicured woodlands, surrounded them. Alecyn made it daytime, wanting to see those houses whose winking lights she found tantalizing. It was Lake Wales.

Rose's face was growing dark with fury. She Sang. The force hit Alecyn like a tidal wave, throwing her to the ground and bringing a warm trickle to her ears. She Sang back, and her Voice was a hurricane. Rose's armor shattered, instantly turning to a fine, black powder that hung around her like smoke. For an instant, Rose stood amid the vaporized armor, a look of pure startlement on her face. Then she herself vanished amid a thick fog.

"I want nothing from him. And I do not want to hurt you Rose. We should fight together. I can destroy him!"

"Nothing can destroy him!"

The voice seemed to come from within the trees, but it was darting as though Rose had become a bird, flitting rapidly from tree to tree. Alecyn felt strong, surrounded by this place. But there was something wrong. A nagging feeling that this wasn't where she was at her strongest.

"Already, he weakens the barriers between our worlds."

"This is your world, Rose! Your name is Rose. A human name! A name of the earth!"

"I am the Black Hand, and I am not of your world!"

"What happened to you that you hate it so much?"

A shape hurtled out of the trees. It was a banshee, the face of a skull, clothed in rags. It reached for Alecyn with arms tipped with talons. And it screamed. Alecyn Sang and held the hideous apparition fast before her. Talons reached for her, mere inches from her flesh. The scream became one of fury. Around them, Lake Wales was disintegrating as the discordant Noise rebounded from Alecyn's shielding to shed the illusion she wove.

"You have forsaken your home too! You have seen the power you can wield in Jonrah. Deny it!"

"I have seen the love that I can have in Jonrah."

"Liar! Jonrah is powerful. I will never be powerless again!"

"I pity you," Alecyn said. Even here, her body unconscious from exhaustion, deep on another plane of being, she could feel the siren song of the Song Fragment. It was becoming part of her, its song ever-present.

Its power waiting to be tapped. Alecyn drew on it now, weaving its alien song into hers and reducing the monster before her to its true human shape. Rose appeared on her knees before Alecyn. She was naked. Covered in welts and bruises layered over old scars. Her skin had a grey pallor. Her hair was brittle and dull. She looked up at Alecyn, and her eyes brimmed with loathing. She held up her left arm.

"Do you see this?" Her finger traced the line of a scar that ran down the length of her forearm.

"This was the first. The very first. And it was not Kragen Onyx who did it to me. It was your world! I was nothing there. I was a victim, and I will not be a victim again. So, strike me down or let me go."

Kill her. It was a voice at the back of Alecyn's mind. A cold, alien tone that whispered to her that this thing before her was an atrocity. It was corruption. She should rid her world of corruption. The voice spoke with such absolute clarity in her mind that it shocked her. The world reeled. Rose was rising to her feet, her obsidian armor intact once again, her face now covered by the blank expanse of her helm. That voice could not be any part of her, surely!

Rose clapped her hands together and unleashed a torrent of pure Noise.

She threw back her head as Alecyn screamed. She felt as though she was being ripped apart, hunched under the onslaught, taken unawares. And the alien voice in her head screamed its rage, howling with insane anger. And then there was silence.

Rose had dropped to her knees, and her head bowed until her forehead kissed the floor. Alecyn stood on a floor of polished black marble. Around her walls became visible, as though a gradual light was dispelling the dark. But she could see no source of light. The chamber was circular, the walls curiously uneven, and they were moving. With horror, Alecyn realized the walls seemed to be made from writhing, moaning bodies. Pain. Pain lashed her. Somehow her back suddenly arched; it had also hit Rose.

Alecyn had felt nothing like it. It wasn't her own pain. It was an agony that emanated from those walls, from the living souls who comprised the architecture of this hellish place. Somehow Alecyn fought the urge to fall to her knees. Her stomach heaved.

"Welcome to the Silence," Rose whispered, and then threw back her head and screamed.

CHAPTER 21:
THE SILENCE

Alecyn screamed. The pain was too great to ignore. It demanded her attention, demanded a response. There was only one she could give. She closed her eyes, tightening them as her mind fled. Sensation fled, and she became capable of only a single awareness, that of the deluge of suffering that bombarded her. Then it was fading. The relief was enough to make her cry out, gasping for breath. Her limbs were like water, incapable of holding her up. Her head throbbed. But she knew this was not the place to be weak. Her physical form was not here, but her mind was. Her soul was. Those who derived their power from the suffering of others had constructed this place to provide strength. Rose was growing stronger. Rose and…

Something was coming. A dread was rising in Alecyn, a fear of the likes of which she had never experienced before. Nausea rose. She wanted to cower. Wanted to run to her father and hide in his strong arms. She wanted to be absolved of leadership and responsibility, to run and hide and not have to be the focus of the terrible thing coming.

"Stand, human." Came the smooth, inflectionless voice.

Alecyn imagined her suit of armor and saw herself in that hard, impenetrable crystal. It strengthened her limbs, allowing her to stand without showing the shaking in her knees.

"Fascinating." said the man who stood before her. He was bald and youthful. His skin was smooth and blemish-free. He had slightly pointed ears and pointed eyebrows, while his lips were full. His floor-length black robe billowed around his waist, revealing his shining black boots. He wore a black tunic that hugged his torso tightly as if it had been poured on him. His head nestled within a high collar. Alecyn recognized the silver and gold inscriptions worked into all his clothes as Song script. He was a Fragment bearer.

"I am Kragen Onyx." He spoke. "Your choice of garb is quite interesting. I wonder if you know what it is, hmmm?"

He moved across the room towards her, looking at her up and down.

"No one has seen such armor in Jonrah since before the War of the Song."

Alecyn didn't know what armor she wore, only that on the Spirit Road, where subconscious impulses were at least as important as conscious ones, this was the protection she had reached for instinctively. But was it protection? She remembered her confrontation with Atramen and how it had seemed to take her over. Something inside had awakened when she had consciously adopted this form, something alien.

"No matter. All will become clear, no doubt. Welcome to the Black Isle." The torture room fell away, walls tumbling into an endless abyss, screams fading with them. The ground under their feet transformed into a stone staircase carved into the side of a mountain. Below, Alecyn could see woods and moors creased into valleys and ridges. Mist hid in the distance except for a single tower, which rose alone on the horizon. Its summit was horned, and a light twinkled there.

"My home," Onyx said, pointing. "I look forward to showing you the Tower in person."

"What do you want of me?" Alecyn managed, fighting to keep her voice even. Rose had transformed into a black panther, which stalked across the floor and was rubbing itself against Onyx's legs. Its purr was a bass rumble.

He idly stroked the big cat with one hand. It reminded Alecyn of Eevee, and she felt a stab of pain.

"So far, you and I have not been direct adversaries. And I thought it was time we talked to make sure that it never occurs."

"Why? You must know I would oppose everything you stand for."

"Do you? I think not." He fixed her with a black-eyed stare. "I seek to restore the world broken apart by the War of the Song. I seek to change the Great Song according to my will. And I am succeeding. Already, the barriers between Jonrah and your world are weakening. If you don't believe me, I advise you to check your…" He cocked his head and pursed his lips. "...phone." He said as though the word was an odd fit for his mouth.

"What do you mean?" Alecyn asked.

"I can send you home. None of this needs to be your problem. Come to me, and together, we can break open the barriers long enough to return you to where you belong."

"You just want this world for yourself. To be a god."

"Yes. Yes, I do." Onyx answered. "And why do you care? I would have no power over you or your world. Go home. Jonrah is not your problem."

She felt relief flooding her at the mere suggestion she could return home and relieve herself of any responsibility for the people of Jonrah. For Jerad. It was the easy way out, and she knew it.

"No, I won't leave Jonrah to you."

Alecyn tried to visualize her home. Her back porch was the one place she knew better than anywhere else in the world. She could smell the freshly painted boards, which she painted in a distinct color every summer.

The gentle sound of a summer breeze in the trees and the glint of sun on water from the lake. But she couldn't change anything around her. Onyx appeared far more versed in control of the Spirit Road than she. He smiled, and suddenly, she felt a familiar vibration coming from her back pocket. Her jaw dropped as she realized it was a ringing phone. Her hands were shaking as she held it in front of her.

It was Abi, her best friend. A fellow nurse at the Lake Wales Medical Center. Her eyes lifted to meet those of Kragen Onyx. He lounged on an elaborate black throne. The panther that had been Rose seemed to have become a large raven perched on his shoulder. His eyes were intent on her. With shaking hands, she pressed the button to hang up the call.

"This is a dream. I know enough about the Spirit Road to know that."

"Is it? Are you sure? I have been walking Deathless Halls since I was a brought here. Do you claim greater knowledge than me? You clearly don't possess greater power."

Alecyn stroked her anger, clinging to the emotion to give her strength. The alien voice was stirring within her. She could not make out its words; they were indistinct, but their tone was clear. Hatred.

"I will never join you or turn my back on my friends. So, you might as well release me. There is nothing you can tempt me with."

"What about your closest friend? The one who came to this world with you?"

The raven cawed, its voice a croaking laugh. Onyx closed his eyes. Tilting his head as though appreciating the grating noise. The world whirled again, but this time, Alecyn felt firmly rooted through the armor that encased her.

"Primitive! Ape! You think you are the master of the higher planes, but you are a child who has learned to run before she can walk!"

Alecyn almost choked. The words were loud in her head. Her throat had tensed to speak them. She had almost shouted them in Onyx's face. But they weren't her words. Something was crawling out of her mind, extending into her limbs, taking over her body. Onyx's eyes bored into her.

Was this him? Did he know?

They were standing in a pool of light surrounded by darkness. All around there were free-standing mirrors. A maze of mirrors. Rose admired herself, as a human, once again. Alecyn turned in a slow circle. She couldn't see her own face.

The crystal armor was opaque, but she found the sight curiously comforting. It felt right. She looked out through the mask as though it wasn't there. Her limbs didn't feel encumbered. She only knew about the armor because she could see it in the mirrors. Then she saw the reflections of Rose, really saw them. In each reflection, the woman was different. In some, the differences were subtle, while others glaring. As the mirrors recede into infinity, the visions became more divergent. Alecyn caught a glimpse in the distance of a scared young woman with a shaved head, wearing a hospital gown, greedily consuming an array of tablets while gulping from a small paper cup.

"What is this?" Alecyn asked.

"My vision of the fractured paths of the future. I imagine that fraud Erevar had his own version. Note how your own form does not change. Not in any future, no matter how improbable. Neither does mine. You and I are universal constants. Do you know why?"

He smiled broadly, clearly enjoying himself. He was correct. Alecyn's crystalline shell remained unchanged in every mirror that reflected her. Onyx, too, looked the same.

"Because we are opposites. You are the Silence, and I am the True Voice. Good and Evil."

Onyx's laughter was like music. It peeled and rolled. It was enticing.

Rose hugged herself, her head rolling back. She looked like a drug addict receiving their fix. Her eyes opened, gazing adoringly at her master.

"That is what the Prophecy is, after all." Alecyn continued.

"The Prophecy! I wrote it!" Onyx continued to laugh. Rose fell to her knees in paroxysms of ecstasy. "And made Erevar think it came from the Waeferen! Hah! The fool! I pulled his strings from the beginning. No, we are unchanged because I sculpted the Great Song to my will, and you created it."

"What are you talking about?!"

"Look at yourself. Human? Does that look human to you, hmmm?" He reached for Rose's chin and turned her face to look at Alecyn.

"No, master. She doesn't look human to me."

"What is she, hmmm?"

"Waeferen, master."

Onyx's smile ignited his black eyes. Alecyn's head whirled. She tried to shed the armor, picturing herself in her jeans and jersey. She imagined the feeling of her favorite sneakers. But the image wavered as the memory was no longer clear. And the shape she saw in the mirror was so much more natural.

"The longer you stay in this world, the more your true nature will overcome you. The more you change. I can send you back. And your little friend."

Suddenly, one person filled all the mirrors.

"Eevee!" Alecyn half sobbed.

She searched for the nearest mirror, reaching for it until her fingers touched the mirror, and it shattered.

"Tut, tut, tut! These portals cannot withstand the mind of someone like you. Be careful. Your friend has become lost in the infinity of possible futures. I can guide her back to the one you inhabit. Send you both home."

As he spoke, his fingers danced in the air as though playing an invisible stringed instrument. Notes tinkled from his movements, a complex melody. In the closest mirrors, Eevee turned to stare out towards them.

"All I ask is that you give up a fight, which is not yours." Onyx continued in a reasonable tone. "And I will return you home together."

CHAPTER 22:
FIGHT OR FLIGHT

Jerad stood for a long time, watching Alecyn sleep. The Kajani who had volunteered to watch over her nestled her into its fur. He found himself frozen for a long moment, wanting nothing more than to stand there. As he turned, he saw Mendel. The Nelim was also watching Alecyn, but his expression was unreadable. His skin was pale, but dark lines chased his cheeks in furious waves. He walked over to Mendel and crouched beside him.

"What's wrong, Mendel?" he asked.

The blue eyes never left Alecyn. His long, thin arms tightened around his knees, which he had drawn up to his chest. "You wouldn't understand." He said shortly. Jerad felt surprised. He had not seen the mystic being rude before.

"Try me." He persisted, making his voice hard.

"Do you know what she did today, human?" Mendel said without looking.

"It was a miracle," Jerad replied.

"The result was a miracle. The method was an abomination."

"Why?"

The Nelim finally looked at him, his face haunted. "There are two ways we use magic, human. We draw it from ourselves, or we draw it from around us. Drawing it from yourself is harder. It takes strength and discipline. Taking it from the world outside is easy. You can perform great works and wield immense power. But it is wrong!"

"How can it be so wrong when she uses it for good?" Jerad asked. He had seen Krissker duck into the tower and look around for him.

"It will change her. She will become like those we fight." Mendel said, looking away. "I can't stand by and watch it happen." Tears were filling his eyes.

Jerad reached out and grasped the Nelim's shoulder. "Then she needs you. More than ever. Right now, she is trying to save all of us, and more besides, the only way she can. She needs you to guide her. None of us can do that." He spoke urgently, wanting to break through the Nelim's despair.

"She may walk a dangerous path, but..."

"Not walking a dangerous path. She avoids a dangerous path and immerses herself in an ocean of peril", replied Mendel.

"Then bring her back." He grabbed both Mendel's shoulders, pulling the Nelim around forcibly to meet his gaze. "That is your job, understand? Stay close to her."

"I don't think I can. I am afraid."

"So am I," Jerad whispered. "But I count you the bravest of us all. You put yourself in danger for her, unarmed. Being afraid doesn't make you a coward. It makes you wise. I need you."

Mendel drew a shuddering breath. The blue lines that swam across his features had slowed and brightened in color, spreading to suffuse his face in a pale, sky blue.

"I will try, Jerad. I will try." He said at last, and then he got to his feet. He walked over to where Alecyn slept and halted within arm's reach before folding his legs beneath him and sitting cross-legged, head resting on his cupped hands. Alecyn's Kajani protector eyed him before flicking a golden-eyed glance toward Jerad. Jerad gave the slightest of nods, and she looked away.

"Your woman will be safe, human," Krissker growled. Jerad started. He hadn't even heard the cat approaching. He forced himself to turn away, mentally shaking himself. This was no time to daydream.

"She's not my woman, Krissker." He said without thinking.

Krissker lifted his head and made the curious coughing laugh, which was Kajani's disbelief.

"I don't need to be human to know the look. You can't hide it."

Jerad stood. He had tried to shut Alecyn out. When they were in the Heart, he had done his best to forget her, telling himself his part in her story was over. But his memories of Alyssa had been a constant needle.

"I had a wife." He replied shortly.

"Wife? Do you mean a mate? Have another." Krissker replied.

"That is not our way. My wife is dead. That is an end to it." Jerad's tone was brutal, knowing the Kajani wouldn't consider it rude. The huge cat shrugged his shoulders, and his whiskers twitched.

"Have it your way. I don't care how miserable you are as long as you fight."

And that's what it came down to, Jerad realized. Alecyn could make him happy. He ached for it. But he knew that if he embraced that longing, it would dull the memory of Alyssa. No longer would she be the last thing he thought about at night. Or the first the next day. No longer would she be the center of his world. It was a wrench that he couldn't bear. It was a betrayal that he couldn't bring himself to accept. But neither could he walk away from

Alecyn. He felt it was tearing him apart, pulling him in two directions.

"Come, we have enemies to deal with. Our scouts have returned." Krissker said.

Jerad nodded and strode out of the tower, and Krissker followed. Outside, Jerad could see through the archway over the gates, down the slope to the tree line. The river pinched together there, creating a bottleneck through which their enemy had to forge a path. At that point, the Nelim and Kajani warriors had erected a barricade and watched the trees beyond warily. A handful of sharp-eyed Kajani prowled the top of the castle walls, too, ensuring that no leaping Mute cut off the defenders on the ground.

Idrasi awaited them beside four Kajani and two Nelim. His face was dark as they crossed the courtyard.

"We lost two of my men," he growled. "We couldn't recover their bodies," he growled. "Too many blasted Mutes. The scouts had no choice but to run."

"What is the situation?" Jerad asked.

Idrasi gestured to one of the Kajani, who held out a forelimb for a wound to be tended by one of the Nelim. She had fiery red fur. Jerad had noticed how those Nelim who had been closer to Idrasi than Vanja had bonded with certain Kajani. This fight seemed to have brought them together in a way he wouldn't have thought possible.

"We scouted the road to the north of here. The one which crosses the river at the ford to the northwest and runs southwest out of the valley."

Jerad mentally orientated himself. Leaving the Tar Valley to the southwest would cross the peat moors, which are desolate but worth building a road years before because of the rich fuel source.

There, it would split with a southern fork, rejoining the Tar at Fearnot. Two days away from the Kajani. Four if burdened with riders, assuming there was enough Kajani for every Nelim, himself, and Alecyn.

"We scouted halfway up the valley side to the hill with the pointed top. We were attacked there by humans heading east. They outnumbered us but had no Mutes with them, and we outran them. But we saw an even larger force to the east of here, coming down from the hills."

"How many?" Krissker asked.

The Kajani screeched loudly as his Nelim counterpart pulled a bandage tightly around her leg. He answered her without looking up from his work.

"Impossible to say at that distance with any precision. But the road was full of them for at least a dozen spear throws that we could see. Choked with the filth."

"They were keeping to the road?" Jerad asked sharply. A nasty thought had occurred to him.

"Yes. They looked like troops marching in good order to me." The Nelim replied.

"Doesn't sound like any Bitterbloods I ever saw," Krissker snarled.

"No, left to themselves, they can be trusted to conduct simple tasks, but they are savages. If they are keeping to the road, it is because there is something with them keeping them in order."

"Every attack we have faced has been a mass assault. No tactics of any kind," Idrasi commented. "So, they have a general?"

"It must be a Shrieker. No simple human could give orders to a Mute, not if he wanted to keep his head on his shoulders."

Krissker gave a long, complicated, rumbling growl, spitting oaths in his native language.

Jerad squatted on his haunches and, with a sharp stone, began sketching on the flagstones.

"We are here. The river is on three sides. Forest all around and roads leading northwest, east, and southwest. Where would you say this force of Mutes is?"

The Kajani placed a paw and a couple of flagstones off to Jerad's right.

"They will be here by dark," she said.

"With a force of humans coming from the west to keep us from fleeing that way."

"We've already seen signs of them, though they keep to the trees," Idrasi told him. "A large force."

"Our choices are limited then. We stay here and hope to hold out until Alecyn is strong enough to transport us away."

"She could transform the Mutes back into their original form," Krissker interjected. "Destroy the enemy in one swipe."

"Assuming the Shriekers can't block her. Or that she can repeat or do what she did here to more than one Mute at a time." Krissker opened his mouth to speak, but Jerad continued. "None of us know the extent of her powers, and she is still learning them. We can't just expect her to wipe out an army of Mutes. We need a backup plan. I would suggest the West. I would rate our chances against humans much higher than against Mutes with magic behind them. We run west and try to cross the Ford at Telthan before the enemy could bar it. Then we run south for Fearnot as fast as we can."

Silence fell over the group. Jerad realized that other Nelim and Kajani had gathered around them to listen. He looked up at the gathered faces, blue-skinned and furred. He met eyes alien to his own but comrades. They weighed his words, respecting his judgment. Would they follow a human?

A low, rumbling growl arose from a few Kajani throats simultaneously.

They rapidly escalated to a brutal roar. Jerad was at a loss how to interpret it, but Krissker was grinning, black lips bearing the full length of his fangs.

"The pride honors you, Jerad. They agree. We run like deer and live to fight tomorrow. Idrasi?"

Idrasi nodded. His eyes shone. "Couldn't have put it better myself, cat," he said, thumping the Kajani's massive shoulder.

Jerad breathed in an inward sigh of relief.

CHAPTER 23:
PREPARING FOR BATTLE

The keep was a confusing mass of activity. They made stacks of weapons according to type: swords, spears, bows, whip-bows, steel claws, spike gauntlets, maces, and axes. Most were Kajani weapons made of heavy steel or ranged weapons designed for a warrior with skilled hand-eye coordination and aim. Each Nelim carried blades, although many fashioned spears or shields using waste wood found in the keep. Hardening the timber to points using fire. Now, all weapons were being pooled to ensure that every warrior left the keep well-armed. It would be enough for the small group in the castle but depressingly little compared to the forces descending on them. The late afternoon sun was falling into the western sky. They saw smoke from the north and west. When the wind was in the right direction, they could hear war chants from human voices. The east was silent.

The time to leave the castle was on them. Jerad checked his own weapons again, reassuring himself for the tenth time of the presence of blades and his whip-bow. Idrasi had his men gathering rocks for slings and scouring the keep for anything else that could be used as a weapon.

Krissker prowled the walls, watching his scouts around the castle and into the trees, looking for any sign of the enemy. Alecyn slept in the tower. Jerad wanted to give her as much time as possible before waking her. He knew enough about magic to know the effort her miracle had taken. He didn't think any of the adepts he had known in the past came near the strength to do it.

A sound came out of the east. It was a scream, as though a titanic beast was howling. Jerad ducked instinctively. He recognized Noise when he heard it. It sent a shudder through the castle walls, causing more than sound to reverberate through Jerad's gut and instinctively causing him to duck. It was a weapon. The walls of the castle shook. Rocks and dust cascaded down. Everywhere throughout the castle, Nelim and Kajani reeled, clutching their ears. He had to see what was happening. He staggered towards the nearest wooden stairs to the wall-top walkway.

Krissker crouched on all fours, his great paws spread and his claws clutching at the stone to maintain his balance. Jerad felt as though his head was about to burst as he lurched against the crenelated battlements, thudding into the stone with a flash of pain.

He forced himself to look out to the east. At that moment, there was an explosion. A fountain of earth and fire erupted from the ground across the river. A shock wave slammed into him, throwing him backward. He would have fallen but for a thick, furred arm that caught him and hauled him beneath the battlements. Jerad and Krissker watched as the blast picked Kajani sentries up and hurled them over the walls like rag dolls. A gout of ancient stone punched outwards, causing the walls to crumble around it, with jagged cracks spattering down from the breach across the courtyard.

The sound cut off abruptly, and Jerad risked raising his head. The crater on the river's eastern bank was wide enough to swallow the castle entirely. It was as deep as the tower was high.

"Warhorn," Jerad said hoarsely. "They have a warhorn. We must go now!"

He staggered to his feet, steadied by Krissker, but feeling as though the ground was moving beneath him. Krissker howled orders in the Kajani tongue. His pride picked itself up. Organizing themselves into two long lines, on all fours, ready for riders. Idrasi was quick to react, a gash on the side of his face ignored as it painted his neck and shoulder with blood. He shouted for his Nelim, and they scrambled to the weapons piles, selecting Kajani weapons and their own, hurling the Kajani weapons to the waiting cats, who snatched them out of the air and into baldrics and sheathes. Vanja and his few remaining followers were also picking themselves up. Realizing they were unguarded; they darted for the gates as one.

A Kajani noticed and poised to spring after them.

"Leave them!" Jerad shouted. "Let them go!"

They all had bigger problems to worry about now. Let Vanja and his traitors meet death the way they wanted. Alecyn appeared at the door to the tower, supported by Mendel. Perseffa loomed behind her, one paw to her side protectively. Her face was pale, and she looked unsteady on her feet. She looked fragile and vulnerable against the dark stone and amid the tumult. Jerad leaped down the rickety steps three at a time, staggering as another terrible cacophony rang across the castle. The ground rippled beneath his feet, slamming him to the ground. He heard Alecyn call out to him and, looking up, saw the stones tumbling from the top of the tower.

"Alecyn!" He screamed. He somehow regained his feet, sprinting towards her, one hand skimming the ground as though he would run on all fours like a Kajani. She stood frozen in the doorway, one hand raised unsteadily to her head. Mendel was looking up. Jerad realized he was too far away to reach her. Perseffa lifted Alecyn at the waist and hurled her forward. The rocks slammed into the space where the Kajani stood, sending stone shards razoring in all directions. Jerad caught Alecyn as she tumbled forward, spinning her to put his own body between her and the collapsing masonry. An explosive energy bursts out with a roar and punches the entire length of the western wall.

Jerad bore Alecyn to the ground, trying to spread himself to cover her as a cloud of stone dust rose from the site of the explosion. Most of the stone flew outwards because of the force of the blast but enough landed to scatter the Kajani and Nelim. The courtyard had loose stones, shattered timbers, and sprawled cats and Nelim. The soldiers took care of clearing the battlements, and the sections of the walls that were still standing looked decidedly unsteady. Cracks rent the stone still standing. In places, it sagged noticeably. Coughing stone dust, he looked up at the tower. The top two stories of the tower were destroyed. The structure leaned precariously to the west.

His eyes found Mendel, staring ashen faced at a chunk of stone twice his size, which had split the flagstones inches from his head.

"Alecyn? Are you well?" Jerad asked anxiously. His body still lay across hers, and he moved to one side, allowing her to turn over. She coughed dust. One side of her face had been scraped, and her clothes had several tears.

"I... I think so..." Her eyes found him. He suppressed a juvenile urge to smile. Next came an overwhelming urge to push himself away from her, to put distance between the two of them. But he didn't. Instead, his arms tightened around her waist, holding her close.

"Jerad!" Krissker roared. Jerad looked up in time to see the massive Kajani throwing off collapsed timber and getting to his feet.

"Here! Idrasi?!" Jerad called.

"Alive!" Idrasi called from the castle gates. Despite his clearly broken hind limb, he grinned through the pain. "I think it's time to follow the traitors' example and get out of here," he said.

Jerad got to his feet, pulling Alecyn up beside him.

"Leave?" she asked. Mendel took her hand, putting a supporting arm under her shoulder. She looked at him momentarily in surprise, then a radiant smile broke over her face, and she accepted the support. Jerad could have kissed the Nelim himself for making her smile like that.

"A force of Mutes is heading this way. Shriekers with them. They are targeting us with a warhorn. We are going to make a run for Fearnot."

"I can do something..." Alecyn began but then slumped against Mendel. Her eyes swam out of focus. "I just need... need... Wait! Where is she?"

Suddenly, Alecyn was awake and alert.

"Who?" Jerad asked, then remembered. "Song! The Mute! The Mute that Alecyn healed! Krissker!"

"We took her to the tower," the Kajani replied.

Alecyn took a step towards the tower, and her knees buckled.

"Mendel. Look after her!" Jerad barked and sprinted for the tower.

He had to climb a haphazard mountain of rubble to reach the entrance. Inside was dark, the stones which had collapsed from the upper floor blocking all the light from above. Rivulets of dust were cascading down from joints in the stone, where enormous blocks shifted against each other. The entire structure was creaking and groaning.

"Krissker, get everyone out of the keep. This thing is going to collapse any minute!" Jerad called.

He dimly heard Alecyn calling to him as he peered into the gloom. Was that a whimper? A female weeping?

"Hello!" He called, then lowered his voice, trying to sound gentler. "Hello? My name is Jerad. We are here to help you. Can you hear me?"

He turned in the dim, moaning darkness. Fallen masonry and jutting timbers were everywhere around him, breaking up the open-plan room into a dozen nooks and hideaways.

"This tower is unsafe. I am here to get you out. We can help you. Please. Just say something so I can find you."

The ground rumbled ominously. There was a wail, an adult voice, but a child's plaintive, fearful cry.

"You're safe now," Jerad said in a hushed tone. "It's all over, come to my voice."

Something moved. A shape stumbled forward, edging closer to him. It was her. Her dark fur hung about her face, laced with dirt. Her eyes were wide and filled with tears. He smiled and reached out his hand. "Take my hand."

The ground rumbled ominously. A spray of rubble slipped through the open doorway from the pile of stones that blocked it. Krissker was halfway down the slope.

"Human! We must go now!" he ordered, sliding to the bottom of the heap and standing framed in the doorway. The Kajani shrieked in fright and backed away.

"No! He is a friend!" Jerad said urgently.

The Kajani female backed into a timber precariously balanced against the wall where it had fallen. It shifted, and a shower of rocks fell from above between her and Jerad. She cowered back, scrambling faster.

"No! Stay where you are. You're making it worse!" Jerad started after her but found himself held by Krissker.

"It is coming down! We need to get out now!" Krissker roared at him.

The Kajani vanished from sight, frantically searching among the debris for a hiding place. Krissker was hauling Jerad towards the door. Jerad fought even as rocks cascaded from above in a continuous avalanche. He was pulled over the masonry pile and placed on the ground on the far side. Behind them, the tower collapsed.

As Jerad picked himself up, a cold fury was blazing inside him. Krissker rose before him, and Jerad reached for his sword before he could stop himself. With a supreme effort, he forced his arm to stop, hand tight on the hilt, muscles bunched and quivering.

"I could have saved her!" he hissed.

Krissker looked at the sword and stepped close to Jerad, spreading his arms wide.

"You would have died trying, human. The needs of the pride are greater than the needs of the individual."

The fury abated. Jerad loosened his grip on the sword hilt. He didn't let go of the anger entirely. But he knew where to direct it. He bowed his head, casting his eyes to the ground, a Kajani gesture of submission. Krissker barked something in Kajani and then was on all fours beside him.

"We are the last human. Let's run!" Jerad clambered astride the Kajani and had barely taken a firm handhold amidst the thick fur.

Then Krissker was bounding out of the gates. The others waited at the barricade, a safe distance from the unstable castle walls. The Kajani riders cleared the barricade in leaps and bounds, riders clinging to their backs with white-knuckled grips. They streamed northwards between the two river channels, making for the pale outline of the road which ran north alongside the Tar. A figure on horseback was emerging from the trees to their right. It cantered forward and then came to a halt. Gloved hands threw back the hood of a cloak to reveal a head that gleamed metallically in the afternoon sunlight. Krissker howled with pure hatred, which erupted simultaneously from every Kajani throat.

It was a Shrieker, Jerad realized. Krissker roared orders, and the line of Kajani curved outwards, away from the solitary figure as far as they could. He himself slowed as he drew level with it. The figure was unclasping its cloak and holding it aloft in one hand, letting the breeze take it. Jerad noticed one side of the cloak was painted white.

"That's a white flag," he said. "That thing wants to talk to us."

CHAPTER 24:
THE ORDEAL

Krissker came to a halt. Jerad stared across the space, separating himself from the evil personified creature. The open ground in front of the castle was a wild meadow. Long grass swayed in the breeze, dotted with the bright colors of wildflowers. The figure which awaited them was a stark contrast to the beauty of nature.

"Perhaps they offer us surrender?" Krissker rumbled.

"Why? Killing us can't present any great difficulty. One Shrieker could wipe us out on its own."

"You're forgetting the Great One, human. They fear her."

"Well, maybe we can make something of that." Jerad mused.

The Kajani that carried Alecyn was turning and racing back down the line towards them. The others had formed an arc, with the Shrieker at the center. Nelim and Kajani stood shoulder to shoulder, weapons drawn. They knew that this could be their end without even the chance to meet an enemy one-on-one. Jerad dismounted from Krissker as Alecyn got unsteadily from her Kajani mount. They were ready. The cat, Jerad, couldn't remember his name, put himself between Alecyn and the Shrieker, which screened her unsteadiness. She looked pale in Jerad's eyes. Her need for rest screamed out. She joined them, Mendel at her back, ready to support her. Jerad hoped he would recognize the need to hide her weakness.

"Shall we?" Alecyn said with a wry smile. She walked towards the Shrieker. Jerad was a step behind her. His arms quivered with their readiness to draw the sword, but he kept his hands away from the hilt. He noticed Krissker's great paws clenching and unclenching, claws whisking in and out. From somewhere behind them, back among the trees, rose a chant punctuated by the hammering of drums. Mutes didn't bother themselves with war chants, and those were Atramen's human forces closing in from the West.

The Shrieker was dismounting and walking towards them, holding its white-painted cloak aloft as it came. When they were close enough to talk, Jerad raised a hand. The Shrieker stopped, letting its cloak fall to the ground. It stood perfectly still, its burnished metal face fixed on them. This close, Jerad could see that there were blemishes on the mask. A crack ran along the left side of the face, and on the right side, a chunk of metal was missing, revealing grey skin beneath. It breathed hard. Jerad wondered what other injuries it hid.

"Well?" Alecyn demanded imperiously. Jerad felt a surge of pride, and there wasn't a tremor of weakness in her voice. "Don't waste our time with demands for surrender. You don't need it, and we will not give it."

"My master does not ask for your surrender and has no quarrel with you, True Voice." The voice was female. It rasped amid a wheezing breath, barely recognizable as a human. "His conflict is with the dark power of the West. Kragen Onyx has manipulated us into war, but he is the real enemy."

The Shrieker suddenly stumbled, one gloved hand clutching at its side as it seemed to fold up its body protectively. It had suffered a wound! Jerad rapidly reassessed the situation. There was another player in this. Someone who could inflict damage on a Shrieker and lead Atramen to...to what? An offer of peace? Alliance, even? The war chants were steadily growing in intensity and volume behind them. A reminder that they had precious little time to deliberate.

Alecyn laughed, stepping closer to the Shrieker. She now stood alone. The creature before her stood far above her, but she seemed taller. She held her head high.

"Since I came into this world, Atramen has been my enemy. He has scourged this land in pursuit of me. We will hold him accountable for that. Does he offer me peace? Speak!"

"He offers your lives and the Southlands in exchange for the Fragment you hold. While you hold it, Kragen Onyx will pursue you and destroy all around you. He offers you a way out of the war against the Silence. If you no longer possess a Fragment, you will not interest my master or Kragen Onyx."

"And let the two of them divide up the world between them? Let Atramen do to another city what he did to Argent?!"

The Shrieker fell to one knee, visibly fighting to rise. One hand was clutching at its side. Alecyn stepped closer again, close enough to touch the creature.

"I intend to put all that he did to the people of Argent right. I intend to take away his army and the Fragment he holds. His days of power are over!"

The Shrieker cried out in pain, raising its arm to protect itself against a blow. Alecyn stood over it, fists clenched, and one raised as though she intended to strike it. Then she whirled as she strode away, though she faltered, stumbling and almost falling. Mendel reached her in a heartbeat before Jerad, supporting her. She regained her feet, swaying momentarily before pushing herself away from the Nelim. The Shrieker hadn't looked up. Jerad backed away from it, hand on his sword now. It stood shakily and raised a hand as it turned back to the trees behind it. A line of Mutes emerged from the tree line.

All along the line, Nelim warriors mounted their respective Kajani, drawing weapons. There came a sudden roar from behind them. Turning, they saw another line of black armored figures emerging from the trees to the northwest. These figures were human, armed with long spears and shields. As they came on, they shouted their war chants and slammed spear shafts into shields. Jerad felt a thrill of fear and embraced it.

Alecyn looked out over the advancing force, then back at the Mutes. The creatures hadn't moved after emerging from the tree line. Faceplates opened and closed. A wash of snarling noise traveled over the intervening distance. They were being held back until the right moment. But why? That many Mutes attacking simultaneously and out in the open would be overwhelming. Why would the Shriekers not unleash them and end the battle as quickly as possible?

"What are they waiting for?" Alecyn asked.

"They seek to let the humans try to destroy us first," Krissker replied.

"They don't want to waste Mutes if they don't have to. Atramen must be losing numbers fast."

Alecyn frowned. "It's the Black Hand. Onyx is waging his own war against Atramen now that he is out from beneath his shield in Argent."

"Atramen is losing." Krissker said, satisfaction dripping from his words.

"So little time!" Alecyn said. "I can help those poor people, but not if the Black Hand slaughters them all."

"Let's worry about our situation first," Jerad suggested. "Krissker, we should forget the Ford and go straight for the river. Due West."

"The current is strong."

"So are your Kajani. Think they could beat the current?"

"Over that distance. Yes. Even with our burdens."

"So, we smash through their line, reach the river, dive in, and keep going. They will not be able to follow us."

Alecyn reached for her flute, and Jerad caught her arm.

"Don't do it. You are not strong enough."

His eyes were met with fierce determination.

"I have to Jerad. I won't let anyone die for me without a fight."

Jerad opened his mouth and drew in a breath. He almost said the words he hadn't spoken since Alyssa; he felt something he hadn't felt for anyone but his wife. Alecyn had not chosen to come to his world. Someone uprooted her and threw her into a place full of horror. And she had fought for herself and those she cared about. Refusing to be intimidated, conquering her fear. A smile touched the corners of her lips as though she had read his mind. She raised the flute to her lips. Jerad drew his sword.

"We're going through them." He said to Krissker. The Kajani bellowed a command, and the others wheeled to the left, forming a wedge with Jerad and Krissker at the point. Alecyn rode in its center. Ahead of them was a sea of black armored infantry. They descended from the forest to the northwest and formed their battle line with their backs to the river.

Those at the front carried long spears and shields; others were visible further back with swords, axes, and hammers. Once the battle started, their line was long enough to surround the Kajani.

As the Kajani advanced, the front ranks lowered their spears, driving the butt into the ground and bracing it with a foot. One Kajani held a spear with both hands, and the next covered him with a shield. The Kajani knew how to fight. Jerad had used the same tactics himself. He knew they would not penetrate that bristling hedge of spear points. Their charge would break against the shield wall and be driven back on the tips of the spears. Kajani would die, and the spearmen would force their riders to fight on foot as they advanced. Even the Nelim, with their extra reach, couldn't reach beyond the length of those spears.

Then he heard the tune. It was played on a single flute, but to Jerad's ears, it soared and thundered as though it rang out from a thousand. All other sounds were silent. The men before them still chanted. Behind the shield wall, men were still beating their shields or armor. The Mutes still lifted their heads, faceplates open. But no sound came from them. At first, Jerad thought it was simply the glorious music drowning them out. Then he saw the fearful looks rippling through the human ranks. They opened their mouths, but no sound came out. Men in the shield wall, who had been hard-eyed and fixed on the advancing Kajani, were now looking around and behind. Confusion spilled through the black ranks.

He risked looking back over his shoulder to where Alecyn rode. Her head lifted, her eyes closed, and she was now producing the music that had started with the flute. There were no words to the Song, and Alecyn's voice was music in its purest form. It wove a tapestry of emotion through the air.

Jerald could feel it lifting him. Nothing could stop this charge. No foe could stand against them. His sword felt light in his hand, and the Kajani were swifter than the wind while their enemy was slow and leaden-footed. A song rose from his throat to join the glorious symphony that suffused the charging Kajani and their Nelim riders. He didn't know what she sang; only that power was flowing through him, as he had never felt. It felt like he had connected to Alecyn. He felt his strength flowing to her while something vastly more powerful came from hers.

He realized that a nimbus surrounded him, all of them. Every movement threw off sparks. He felt he could tear down mountains, and as his exaltation rose, so did the song that poured from him. The Kajani sang, too, their voices raised to the winds. Before them, the first lines were lowering their spears. Jerad could see the panic setting in as the song of their foe reached them. He saw men push back into the ranks behind, then turn and run.

Krissker hit the first rank in mid-leap with his front paws outstretched. Men fell to either side like wheat before a scythe. Jerad shouted wordlessly as he hacked left and right with his sword. The Kajani wedge slammed into the human warriors and mowed them down. Where men had been running, they now cowered on the ground, weapons forgotten. The Kajani ignored them, bounding onward towards those who stood their ground. Jerad knew the moment that Alecyn had lost consciousness. Suddenly, the Song was over. The surrounding nimbus was gone, and the sounds of battle was once more predominant.

The Kajani advance had slowed to a walking pace now. They used teeth and claws to carve a path through the warriors before them while their riders lashed out to the sides. Jerad looked around to see Alecyn being carried in the arms of her Kajani mount. Others clustered around them, facing outwards in all directions to protect Alecyn. In the middle, alongside her, was Mendel. His mouth moved, but his sounds were lost amid the battle. But the ground erupted beneath the feet of those who came too close. Warriors were plucked from their feet by invisible hands and flung high into the air.

A Mute landed in front of him. Another came from the sky, landing too close to Krissker and dying instantly as a limb the size of a tree trunk lashed out. More Mutes were landing amid the Kajani formation. They had pursued from the east and were now leaping, descending amid their human allies. Faceplates opened, and Noise poured out. Krissker flinched away, and a spray of blood spat into the air. He charged, tramping the Mute and bending his head to rip out its throat. Something hit the two of them from behind with the force of a hammer, and Jerad was falling. He rolled and strove to regain his feet, slashing aside spear thrusts. Krissker, one side of his face dark with his own blood, wrestled with two Mutes, which clung to his massive body like leeches.

Everywhere Jerad looked, the Mutes were overwhelming the Kajani by the sheer weight of numbers. There was no way out. He stabbed at the mute clinging to Krissker, impaling it and hurling it aside. A dagger thrust into an open faceplate, dispensed with a second. Krissker's claws spilled organs from the torso of a third. But the sky was black with them. Even their human allies were fighting them, finding hungry Mutes within their ranks, unleashing Noise indiscriminately. Jerad felt pain lancing through his head as if someone had stabbed him in the ears with a poniard. He felt a warm trickle painting the side of his face as his ears bled. He fought on.

Krissker was staggering to where his kinsmen protected Alecyn with their bodies. One arm hung uselessly at his side, and blood darkened his fur. Jerad fought to gain his side, but his boots slipped on the ground and churned into red mud. He fell to one knee as a Mute fell onto Krissker's back. It reached around, flourished, and drew its taloned hands across the Kajani's throat. Blood poured out, and Krissker was down.

Jerad screamed and found his feet. He leaped from a fallen Kajani, snatching up a whip-bow and lashing it outwards in the same movement. He caught the Mute around its head, whirling towards him, as he released the whip and swung back his sword. The stroke took off the Mute's head.

But it was too late. As he gained Krissker's side, he saw the ravaged gash that had been his throat. Open eyes stared blindly. Kajani were down all around. Alecyn and her protectors were invisible amidst ten times their number of Mutes. Jerad's arms felt as though he could never lift them again. Despair hung on him like lead. Exhaustion dragged at his feet. He couldn't reach her in time. After all this, he couldn't save her. The enemy was going to win. For the second time, Atramen would take away the woman he loved. No! No! Nooooo!

A scream of despair rose within him as he gripped his sword in two hands and lurched to his feet. Pain lanced through his limbs as he raised the blade and prepared for one last fight. A mute died as metal hissed through the air and bisected it. Jerad pulled the sword free and moved on to the next. Two slashes and the creature fell. Claws raked his shoulder, but the pain was secondary to his need to reach Alecyn. He could no longer hear anything from the left side, where a painful whistle was drilling into his head. Something was wrong with his right leg. It was too heavy to move, and he couldn't bear his weight. He adjusted his stance and fought on.

A Mute faced him, knocking aside his sword arm to step in close and clutch his throat in one clawed hand. He punched at the armored face until his knuckles were bloody, but the Mute squeezed, and his vision darkened. Something plucked the Mute off its feet and flung it high into the air. There was a familiar sound, a keen screech. And then a stormbird was barreling through Mutes and humans alike, raking its enormous talons through them as though fishing. It rose gracefully, blood raining from the bodies it clutched, squeezing them tight before releasing them to plummet to the ground. Jerad couldn't stand. He crawled towards the last place on the field where he had seen Alecyn. More stormbirds were descending. They came down in waves, clearing vast swaths of the field. As he reached Alecyn and clutched her hand, he was dimly aware of one of the giant birds settling on the ground not far away. Then consciousness fled.

CHAPTER 25:
RETURN TO FEARNOT

Alecyn walked the Spirit Road. It was becoming second nature. There was no confusion as she looked down at her unconscious body. She knew she had spent all her body's energy on that last act of magic. She had pulled energy from humans, Kajani, Nelim, and Mute alike. From the trees and the depths of the earth. It had raged in her, a frenetic burning mass of magic that demanded to be acted upon. And from her had come the Song, to give strength to those who fought for her and weaken their enemies. But even as she had drunk the energy of the surrounding life, she had drained herself. The very act of crafting that complex Song had drained her dry. It had been like boring a hole in the Hoover Dam. Once unleashed, the power flooded from her.

Jerad crawled to her as the giant birds rained vengeance on Atramen's armies. She could see three Shriekers fleeing into the trees to the east. They hadn't even joined the battle, conserving their strength and clearly hoping that the onslaught of the Mutes would subdue her. She reached for them on Spirit Road casually. The understanding of how to do it was just there. Their minds were dark, diseased, and corrupted jewels. That corruption stained the Spirit realm, leaking out in ripples. She felt a moment's revulsion as she reached through that stain to grasp the mind of one of them.

It stopped. Alecyn caressed the warped mind and then drew it to her. The Spirit form of the Shrieker appeared before her. She had drawn them both to her own island of security. She sat on the bench on her porch in Lake Wales. The sun was setting, and the air was cool. Cicadas buzzed reassuringly. She smiled and stretched. She wore her PJs, light cotton pants, a vest top, and fluffy socks.

The Shrieker would have drawn stares in the real Lake Wales. There was no one to stare at unless Alecyn conjured them. She looked unflinchingly at the unmasked face. Its skin was grey and pocked with dark scabs. One side had fallen as though it had melted. She pitied the creature. She thought it had once been male. It lifted its hands to cover its face, crouching before her and making panicked animal noises.

"Where is Atramen?"

Suddenly, a map of the Southlands stretched across the porch boards between them.

"Your army is lost. I have the means to restore all those foul Mutes he created. And I doubt your human allies will stay loyal once we defeat that force. Tell me where I can find him."

Her tone was cruel. Too much depended on this pathetic excuse for a sentient being. She had to consider the bigger picture. If she could reach Atramen, she knew she could destroy him completely. With every use of the Song Fragment, the next seemed easier. The Great Song was seeping into her, making itself part of her. Or...no, it had always been there, but she had hidden it under her human identity. Now, someone removed that cover, exposing her true nature. The Great Song was part of her, in her DNA. The true Alecyn.

"Shall I heal you of the scourge that afflicts you?" Her skin glittered as though covered in diamond dust. "I can do it. I can heal your twisted mind and make you whole again."

The Shrieker prostrated itself before her, stretching its arms to her.

"Please!" it implored through its distorted mouth. "Please, Great One!"

Humans! So lacking in vision and strength! These children had sought to harness the power of the world around them, and it had warped them like candle wax. But she herself was human. Wasn't she?

"Where is he?"

"He hides... from the Black Hand. In the mountains to the north!"

Alecyn raised an eyebrow, lifting her feet to escape the creature's touch.

"Show me!" she commanded, putting power into her voice.

The Shrieker scrabbled on the map, which covered the floor. Then, it pointed at a spot in the middle of the range, which divided eastern Jonrah into north and south. It is almost due south of Argent.

"The temple of Ishein!" It blurted. "He hides amid the ruins of the temple!"

It suddenly convulsed, blood erupting from its mouth. Its limbs spasmed as though it had lost all control of its body. It jerked upright, eyes open and staring, but somehow empty. A deeper voice came from its grey lips now, one she recognized.

"I will tear the Fragment from your dead hands! My creatures will relentlessly scourge your lands until they convert every human! I will squeeze the life from your throat with my bare hands if necessary!" Atramen roared. But Alecyn could hear the tinge of panic in that once powerful voice.

Alecyn raised an eyebrow. "Then why are you hiding, Great One?" She replied, her tone mocking. "I will come for you in good time. Or I will make an alliance with the Black Hand. We are both from the same world. While you cower in hiding, all your enemies will unite against you!"

The Shrieker exploded, its spirit form becoming dust that flew everywhere. Alecyn hoped her taunting would achieve the desired effect. Atramen needed to be desperate to destroy her. He needed to be reckless. She looked at the sunset, pondering. The lake was gold, slashed with red blood.

The sun was below the horizon. Its colors a riot of splendor. It didn't please her as it once had. She reached down from her seat absently. It was only when she didn't feel Eevee's fur that she remembered. Eevee was not here. Eevee went missing. But now she knew what to do about that. She had broken the anchor that held Eevee to her own place in the complex symphony that was the totality of existence. She lost herself in time, unable to find her way back to where she belonged without help.

Alecyn smiled a broad smile of expectation as the flute materialized in her hands. Grandpapa's flute. The ancient Irish instrument whose voice spoke of so many distant lands and stories. As a child, she had wanted to know all of them, all the songs, all the stories. Well, now she could. Everything existed within the Great Song. It was everything, and everything was It. And she knew the Great Song. It resonated within her. She played.

The tune she played had no name and was unlike anything anyone had ever heard before. It looped and spiraled across the Spirit Road, transcending limiting concepts like worlds. Its melodies reverberated amid spiral clusters of stars and danced amid dense black depths of void at the furthest reaches of creation.

It was a beacon that shone beyond Jonrah, Earth, and time. The Song shone outwards, reaching those who could recognize and understand its siren call. Her skin's diamond glitter deepened, and a rainbow of color shone out from her body as she lost herself in the music.

"So, you know, do you?" A familiar voice came, and Alecyn laughed aloud as she leaped to her feet and flung herself to the porch railing.

Eevee stood below, walking up the path from the lake to Alecyn's desert garden backyard. She wore a simple dress of white cotton, and her hair was short and spiky. It was also pure white. She glowered at Alecyn.

"I can see from that ridiculous display that you are embracing your heritage. Well, you can stop that Noise this instant, young lady!"

Alecyn had stopped, but only because it was impossible to maintain such music while her insides were leaping with childish excitement.

"Eevee!" She laughed and wept simultaneously, jumping three steps, and sprinting down the path. "You're alive! I brought you back! I brought you back!"

"Yes, you did. I didn't think it was possible. You are the only being in the world with the power to send out a beacon like that. Do you know how many timelines you have rewritten with your... your... shouting?"

"I don't care! I don't care! You're back, and I know how to stop Atramen! Eevee, everything is going to be ok?"

"Really, child. Have you looked at your own inner vision of yourself?"

Eevee was pushing Alecyn away and holding her at arm's length. "What do you look like?"

"Waeferen," Alecyn said, holding up her shining arms. "Or at least half-Waeferen. I am a hybrid, Eevee. Just like you."

"Nothing like me. My mind is a forced blend of Waeferen and cat. If you ask me, the result of the actions of a headstrong Waeferen. You have Waeferen blood in your heritage, too. God in heaven, I don't know what you're becoming."

"I'm still me, Eevee. I will always be Alecyn. On the physical plane."

"The physical plane! Down there, I am just a cat. You should know by now that Spirit Road is where we are our true selves. If you will wield this power, you need to learn to control it."

Alecyn could only laugh. She had Eevee back. The shimmer on her skin and the strange voice that whispered in her head when she walked the Spirit Road didn't concern her. She was in command of this power that had awakened inside her. She breathed it as naturally as air. There was nothing she couldn't do with it. Eevee's face darkened, and suddenly she was transforming. Before Alecyn's eyes, she became a cat and leaped. Her paws struck Alecyn's chest with more force than her slender feline form should ever have had. Alecyn felt herself overbalanced, and then she fell. She fell through the world. Lake Wales toppled away from her. The battlefield flew past her. She awoke.

****

She sat upright with a gasp of indrawn breath. She was in a white-painted room. Soft cotton sheets fell away from her. Beneath them, she was wearing a nightdress. Sunlight streamed through windows that looked out into a blue sky. Eevee was curled up next to her. She fixed Alecyn with a languid, green-eyed stare and got up, hopped off the bed, and stretched.

"Good morning to you." The voice was soft and warm. It belonged to a middle-aged woman with long dark hair, which lay over her shoulder in a braid. She offered Alecyn a glass of water. She was sitting in a simple, white-painted wooden chair.

"Morning. Where am I?" Alecyn asked.

"Fearnot. We brought you into one of our healing houses unconscious, although I could not find any wounds on you. My name is Aoife."

"I'm Alecyn."

"I know. Your friend Mendel told me." Aoife pointed to a pallet in the corner where Mendel's tall, angular figure stretched out and was fast asleep. "You were exhausted. And so was he. He quickly fell asleep once he discovered that you weren't harmed."

Alecyn smiled fondly. She got out of bed and padded across the room to him. She knelt beside his makeshift bed and ran a hand across his head. His eyes fluttered open, and she smiled down at him.

"Hello, sleepy." She said.

"Hello, Alecyn." He replied groggily.

"Thank you for coming back to me, Mendel," Alecyn said, leaning down to embrace him. He returned the hug awkwardly, and Alecyn realized she didn't even know if this was a Nelim practice.

"I couldn't abandon you, Alecyn. You're... you are my friend." He took her hand and turned it gently into the light from the window. A faint glitter could be seen. He met her eyes. "If you will have me, I will still guide you in this."

Alecyn nodded. "Provided you accept, there are things I must do." She said seriously. Mendel nodded.

"I still hope to persuade you of the wrongness of your approach, though."

"How many of the others survived?" Alecyn asked, turning to Aoife. She remembered the desperate battle, the carnage as the Kajani had fought to protect her. Fought and died.

"The storm riders brought back six. Three of them... Nelim, and three Kajani." Aoife clearly struggled with the unfamiliar names.

"And Jerad?" Alecyn knew he lived. She had heard his Song while she walked Spirit Road. In fact, she could hear it now, she realized.

It was a faint tune. As if she had heard something carried in the wind from far off. She hummed along with it, gently repairing broken or discordant sections as she heard them. She knew that somewhere, some of Jerad's hurt had disappeared. The Song grew stronger. She enjoyed hearing it and liked the feeling of intimacy with him.

"He was badly wounded, but I think he's going to pull through."

"He is," Alecyn said with certainty. "Are you the healer?"

"We call it Pathfinder. And yes, I play the harp, which is on the green. And I use it to help those who need it.

"You did an excellent job with Jerad. His Song is whole and regaining its strength."

Aoife hesitated before replying. "So, you are the one?" she finally asked. "The one that Jerad and Lucas went to Argent to find? The…"

"True Voice?" Alecyn laughed. "I would never claim a title like that, but... everyone thinks I am. I want to do what I can to help people. I was a... healer back home. Now, Aoife. I feel refreshed. I would like to see Jerad."

Aoife produced clean clothes for Alecyn from a cabinet beside the bed. They were simple but comfortable: a dark blue wool dress with sturdy ankle-high boots and a coat. She wished her jeans had survived this far, but she supposed that after the miles of mud, sweat, and blood they had to endure, they would be beyond even the best laundry in Jonrah to restore. The house, along with a dozen others, stood in an area of the city that had been burned down during the siege.

Aoife had recommended to the Governor that buildings were needed to house the sick and injured. As they descended a plain wooden staircase that looked like brand-new wood, Alecyn saw other white-painted houses through a window. Beyond them, in the distance, a wall rose that seemed to have been made from large chunks of mountain stone. Aoife told her much about Fearnot, often referring to it as the village and having to correct herself. It was a city now, with many refugees who had arrived from the countryside fearing leaving. She talked about the Governor, seeming to think highly of him. To Alecyn, it sounded like this governor ruled Fearnot as a king in all but name.

"I will need to speak to the Governor, Aoife," she said.

"Of course. And I am sure Lucas will want to speak to you now that you are up and about. He has been to see you and Jerad many times. He led the stormbirds that rescued you."

****

She opened a door and entered a room almost identical to the one she had woken in. It was well lit, with sunlight spilling through generous windows. There was little furniture other than a bed. Jerad was lying in that bed. Bandages were wrapped around his face, shoulder, and arm.

Alecyn looked at him for a long time, standing at the end of his bed. Once again, he tried to put his body between her and harm. He had risked all saving her. When they were done, would he want to return to his home? They had talked a lot since their meeting, and his fondness for Fearnot had shone through. Alecyn walked to one of the windows and looked out. This side of the building looked away from the other Healing Houses. Everywhere she looked was new construction. Houses are being built. It truly was a city.

"How does it look?" Jerad asked.

Alecyn spun to see Jerad watching her, a tired smile on his face.

How are you feeling," she asked.

"I feel surprisingly good, given how much pain I was in the last time I awoke. Your handiwork?"

Alecyn blushed. She rushed to the bed, and only when she reached it did she stop, suddenly awkward. Aoife quietly placed a chair beside her and excused herself from the room. Alecyn put a gentle hand on Jerad's chest, softly stroking. Her heart was racing, and her breath was short. "It is getting easier. I could hear your Song from upstairs without even needing to search it out. And the healing was as easy as breathing. I could heal everything..."

"No. Save your strength." Jerad put a hand on hers. "You are going to need it. Atramen is still out there."

Alecyn nodded. "I do not think you will recognize your home, Jerad. From what Aoife had told me, the war has changed it beyond recognition."

"War does that. But this is not my home. Argent was where I was born. Where I got married. Fearnot brought me back to life after losing Argent. It gave me a purpose. At the time, I needed that more than anything."

"And now? What is your purpose now?"

"The same as it has been all along. To see you safe."

"And the Silence ended?"

"To see you safe," Jerad insisted.

"I was worried that you would want to stay here. You rescued me. And now you are home, and there is plenty to do here. I was worried you would not want to come with me."

His hand tightened on hers. "I wouldn't abandon you, Alecyn." He looked into her eyes. "I thought you would want to go home yourself."

"No. I couldn't abandon you either." On an impulse, she leaned in and kissed him. An embarrassed cough broke the two apart. Mendel stood by the door, clearly torn by agonies of embarrassment. Alecyn had entirely forgotten him.

"Aoife asked me to tell you. There is someone here to see you." The Nelim said, looking at the floor and flushing a deep, dark blue. A young man with a round face and short, dark hair entered the room. He wore a distinctly military-looking uniform that had clearly been patched together simply from ordinary garb, dyed a uniform grey, and then someone stitched an emblem in the shape of a bird with wings spread wide to the shoulder. He fastened a sword to his waist and inserted thick leather gauntlets through the sword belt on the opposite hip.

"Sorry to interrupt. I had word that you were awake, Miss Alecyn. May I come in?"

"Lucas!" Jerad exclaimed. The young man beamed as he entered. Jerad struggled to sit up and clasped his hand.

"Jerad! Great Song, but it is good to see you again! You will not believe what we have done while you were away!" The young man gushed.

"Alecyn, this is Lucas Haverford." Jerad introduced.

"Lucas, this is Alecyn Johnsenn. She is the one we went to Argent to find."

Lucas bowed formally. "My lady. It is my pleasure to welcome you to our city. Finding you was quite the adventure for Jerad and me."

"I'm glad to be here, Lucas," Alecyn replied. "You can help. I need to speak to the Governor. I have a plan that will destroy Atramen's entire army of Mutes. But I am going to need help to put it into place."

"I am the Governor," Lucas said. "And whatever help we can give is yours."

Jerad flopped back onto the bed. "You? You are leading the Council. How did you get Avery to agree to that?"

Lucas' fresh-faced enthusiasm fell away. "He did not. The Council has been dissolved. You do not know what it was like here. Fresh refugees are coming in daily, more than we could feed or house. Mutes are raiding closer. The Council could not manage it. They froze. I took control. I started giving orders, and people followed them. I have been giving orders ever since."

Jerad nodded, understanding. "I can't imagine certain others going along with that easily."

"Avery was the worst. Seth and Asher followed him. They were going to do something that would have been incredibly dangerous. I had our militia behind me."

"So, you took control by force." Jerad finished.

"I had Avery, Seth, and Asher all imprisoned. They were trying to negotiate with the enemy. It could not go on." He looked at Jerad anxiously. "Do you hate me?"

Jerad shook his head solemnly. "You did what you had to do for Fearnot."

"After I killed the Shrieker, they were released. But Avery would not relent. He kept conspiring, kept resisting." The pain was visible on Lucas' face.

"He tried to raise a revolt among the people of Fearnot against me and the refugees. I... I executed him by hanging." Jerad held his gaze for a long moment. Something passed between the two men that Alecyn could not follow. Her heart went out to the young man who had bounded into the room to greet Jerad like a puppy. The burdens on his shoulders were almost tangible.

"You did what you had to do," Jerad repeated. "You are responsible for everyone's safety now. You have a greater good to protect."

Lucas nodded, but a haunted look filled his eyes.

"What do you need from us, Alecyn?" Lucas asked finally.

"I have a Song that will heal the Mutes, but I need to reach as many of them as possible at once. Atramen will come for me with everything he has. They will come here. I need to reach all of them at once with my Song."

"A warhorn," Jerad said. "Atramen has them. We could use it to broadcast the Song. We would need to capture one."

"Do you have enough men to do that?" Alecyn asked Lucas.

He grinned. "Yes. Because I have already done it. Three times, to be exact. The Stormriders captured them in a raid about a week ago. It cost us dearly to hold them while we moved them to the city walls, but we got them here."

"That is the answer then. We use the weapon of the enemy against him." Alecyn said.

CHAPTER 26:
THE TRUE VOICE SINGS

Alecyn stood atop one section of Fearnot's extraordinary wall and marveled. She felt like she was standing on top of a mountain. The rock was triangular, with the beginnings of steps painstakingly carved out of two sloping sides. Its irregular upper edge had become a makeshift battlement with men looking out over the lands to the east, ever watchful.

A rope, knotted into hand and footholds, dangled over its precipitous front face, and far below was one of the three warhorns that Lucas' men had paid so dearly to capture. She surprised herself by feeling no vertigo, standing atop the rock above the city. The tallest of the new houses being built in the city reached only halfway up the boulder. Others lay on either side and in a long curving line to north and south. The Mountain Walls was the name the men gave to them.

"Great god in heaven, girl, you're not thinking of climbing down, are you?" Eevee almost screeched.

"Yes," Alecyn replied. "I must be at the mouthpiece of the horn. And so will you. Mendel will man the northern horn, you the southern. You will have to climb down the walls to reach it."

"I know! I know! I am a cat girl. I land on my feet, but there is a limit. This is a foolish plan."

"It will work. Your music, magnified by the horn, will join with mine. And I will shape it to my purpose."

"Is there even enough human left? I know! You did it once. But I talked to Jerad, and that girl was far from... well... normal. She was almost childlike according to him."

"I know where I went wrong. Her Song was imperfect. I can correct that mistake."

"You are experimenting with these people, Alecyn. How does that make you any different to Atramen?" Eevee leaped to the battlement in cat form and skipped from one stone outcrop to another.

"Because I am doing it to save them all. To make them human and free."

"And then what? Use them as an army to liberate Argent, I suppose."

Alecyn waited to answer. "I will not use anyone. I will end Atramen. Then anyone who wishes to return to Argent may do so."

Eevee retraced her steps until she was level with Alecyn.

"Mendel is worried about you. He says you will lose yourself if you continue down this road."

"Enough!" Alecyn snapped. "I do what must be done. Now, go take your place, Eevee."

The cat stayed where it was, watching her with unblinking green eyes.

"Please, Eevee. I need you." Alecyn finally implored.

Eevee stroked herself past Alecyn's ankles as she padded away to the south.

Alecyn swung herself over the battlement and, taking hold of the rope, climbed hand over hand to the wooden scaffold erected around the warhorn. The horn, as wide across as a bus, was made of stone.

It stood easily as tall as a two-story house. Behind the vast construction was a wooden platform and a complex metal, wood, and stone arrangement arranged in a spherical shape. It had an opening at one end and another on the opposite side. Inscriptions and runes crawled across every available inch, as they did on the surface of the warhorn itself.

Jerad stood, examining the enormous weapon. He could not descend from the walls, so he had ridden out of the southern gates and around the walls. Jerad clutched a staff to aid his walking and moved one arm sparingly, wincing with pain. He had refused her offer of healing and made it clear he would be angry if she wasted even a note of magic on him. She had eased his pain, though his flat looks suggested he knew what she did. Lucas stood next to him, leafing through parchments marked with scrawls of charcoal writing. They were the reports from his storm riders of enemy movements.

"This time, I think we're in business," he said. "Reports of open movement of Mutes on the main roads from the north and south. No attempt at stealth and moving this way at speed. They are leaving behind their human infantry and even their own warhorns. There will be twenty thousand here by midnight tomorrow. Are you sure you can operate this? We have not been able to make heads nor tails of it."

"Yes, I can operate it," Alecyn said, lost in examining the spherical construct. She did not know what it was, but somewhere within her memory, there was a tug of familiarity, and she knew if she could let her mind relax, the answer would come to her. Something within her told her this was a primitive version of a more sophisticated artifact that had never existed in this world. But she knew its operating principles and of what it was capable.

"Alecyn... your skin." Jerad began worriedly.

"I know. Please do not worry. I know what I am doing."

Alecyn understood as she sought to bring out those alien thoughts and memories her body was responding to. Her skin was gleaming and glittering, brighter. It no longer bothered her. The Music was all. She Sang. Light flickered through the inscriptions around the sphere in pulsing waves. A glow began from within, and then... A sound erupted from the horn itself. It passed across the ground, cleared from the forest before the walls, and hit the trees like a wave. As it passed, a blossoming of new growth appeared. Blossom and fruit festooned branches. Butterflies and bees hovered around the new growth in clouds. Even the grass before the trees looked lusher and greener.

Alecyn stepped back with a smile. "Successful test," she said. Lucas stared at her, open-mouthed. Jerad smiled proudly.

At that moment, a Noise erupted from the trees, sounding like a thousand lost souls screaming from the deepest pits of hell. Alecyn whirled in time to see a crack in the sky above the trees. A jagged, snaking flash of lightning widened, tearing apart the sky to reveal an emerging black swarm.

"Mutes!" Alecyn shouted. "They're here!"

The creatures spilled from the expanding crack. They hit the ground in fountains of earth to leap skyward again, coming forward in huge bounds.

The torrent seemed unending, filling the sky. Lucas was moving before the first Mute emerged. He leaped for the rope to ascend the walls, but Jerad stopped him.

"Do not be a fool, man! Your men know their orders. You will be picked off that rock before you get halfway!"

Lucas shook him off with a snarl, but Jerad grabbed the front of his tunic. "Use your head, Governor! You cannot help your men if you are dead!"

Alecyn was aware of the tableau on the periphery of her consciousness. She ascended to the Spirit Road and sought Mendel and Eevee. Both were in place, surrounded by Lucas' best Stonemen. She touched their minds, giving them reassurance.

"Mendel, my friend. Be steadfast. I trust in your courage more than anything else."

Mendel smiled. "Even if it ends here. I have lived more in the last months than most do in a lifetime."

"I'm ready, Alecyn," came Eevee's voice. "I will give you a song that will make your feet itch. You use it well, girl."

Alecyn returned to her body. A cadre of Stonemen had taken a position with her, Jerad, and Lucas at their center. They carried spears, shields, and bows and had the look in their eyes of men prepared to die.

Alecyn took her position and waited.

"They are over the walls. Do it!" Lucas urged.

"Not yet. I want them all through that portal first." Alecyn told him calmly.

The crack in the sky was still spilling black, swarming shapes, but the flow was lessening now. A detached part of her mind could distinguish the music that formed the heart of that breach. It was a breach, a tear rather than a portal. She could see a way of making that Song better and more effective. It must be draining Atramen's strength in its present form, even with a fragment.

She held her own Fragment closely, feeling its warmth against her stomach as she stood with her arms wrapped around it. Mutes were landing on the warhorn and its scaffolding. Lucas was shouting orders, and bows were springing into action. Arrows with thick shafts and armor-piercing points hurled away mutes. More whined into the air, distracting the creatures. Still, Alecyn waited. There was a scream close by, followed by heavy blows on wood. The surrounding men were closing ranks, slamming their shields, and thrusting spears outwards to drive off attackers.

She knew men were dying. Knew that the longer she waited, the more Mutes could breach the walls. She knew people were going to die. But she needed to take them all. She would end this with one blow. Alecyn Sang. A heartbeat later, two more Songs rang out from the north and south. Alecyn drew her power from the Fragment and those glorious symphonies of magic. She pulled more than ever, drawing on Jonrah's deepest, most secret power reserves. Every living thing within the walls stopped for an instant as she drew its energy to herself.

Then her Song poured out of the warhorn. It was a wave of music. It cascaded outwards across the hordes of Mutes. One could observe the waves of music progressing outward. Trees bent before it momentarily as though in the presence of a shock wave. But it was the Mutes who felt its effect the strongest. As one, they slowed their actions, whether charging towards the human defenders or battling them. Heads lifted as the music swirled invisibly around them. Men faced a defenseless enemy. The Mutes lowered their arms and stood silent and still. They held back their vengeful sword blows, hearing the music and knowing it signified something remarkable.

Within a brief space of time, the battle had ceased. Men lifted the visors of their helmets and lowered their shields. Jerad and Lucas did not notice the cessation of the fighting. Jerad and Lucas were in awe of Alecyn. She blazed white. Her skin shone brilliantly white. Her eyes were coruscated. Jerad reached out to her, but Lucas held him back. His mouth worked furiously, but no sound came from him. There was no sound anywhere except the Song that Alecyn wove. Now, a light was growing among the Mutes. It was blurring their outlines, distorting their monstrous shapes. The black armor of their skin was lightening, becoming soft. They were becoming recognizably human.

Alecyn bathed in power. She felt like a goddess. Nothing could be beyond her. Her awareness expanded with the Song, riding its sound waves into the world. She could feel the Songs of every individual there in Fearnot. She felt it was not beyond her to stretch further, leave Fearnot behind, and allow her mind to expand to the Black Isle.

Surely, with this much power, even Kragen Onyx could not stand against her. No! That was not her purpose. Not yet. With an effort of will, she pulled herself back to Fearnot. The Mutes were a cacophony of ruined and distorted music, almost unbearable to hear. She corrected it. Her Song repaired theirs, bringing them back into tune and rhythm where they had been Noise and Chaos before. She felt the rightness of it. Like a master player fine-tuning an instrument, hearing it move from jarring atonal notes to perfect pitch.

She did not need to see the effect to know her Song was working. The Songs spoke for themselves. She could also see where she had gone wrong with her first attempt to heal a Mute. She had left the Song unfinished in a crucial area. Now, she corrected herself and even improved on the original. She was a goddess! The people about to awaken from their long nightmares would all possess the capacity for greatness. They would rebuild Argent and make it a city of story and song.

"Do not overreach yourself, girl! Do not lose yourself. You are half-human, remember!" came Eevee's voice. It sounded distant, Eevee's mind speaking to her through the glorious symphony of power that Alecyn wove. "Focus, now!"

Eevee was right. Alecyn reluctantly wove her Song to its conclusion. The music faded and ended. Silence reigned. It was the stunned silence of people who had seen the gods come down and walk among them. It was the silence that followed. Across Fearnot but mostly concentrated in the open ground between the mountainous walls and the forest, were unconscious, naked men and women where once there had been Mutes. Alecyn's voice rang out across the city.

"Help them! They are your siblings. No longer are they the enemy. They are like you but far from home. They are like children. Vulnerable and afraid, waking from a terrible, dark sleep. Help them."

Silence. Stillness. Then, a soldier with a scarred face dropped his sword and knelt to pick up the young woman who had been a demon seeking to tear his throat out just a moment before. He made his way towards the Healing Houses. Aoife was bustling out of one of them, sleeves rolled and leading a phalanx of healers and helpers.

"You heard the Lady. These people need our help. Jenn, they are going to need clothes. Garments from every house, anything you can lay your hands on. Sara, blankets, we need blankets. Everyone else can go without. Come on, now!"

Another soldier cradled a crying young man in his arms, stroking his hair and whispering that he was safe, that the ordeal was over. The people of Argent were awakening from their nightmare, and the people of Fearnot were there to help them.

Alecyn looked up at the crack in the sky through which the Mutes had descended. She felt weakened but had a last reserve of strength available to her. One last effort!

"You did it!" Jerad had tossed away his crutch and cannoned into Alecyn, lifting her with his one good arm, pressing her body to his. He spun her, then putting her back on her feet, cupped her face gently. "Great Song! But you did it!"

"It's not over yet, Jerad," Alecyn replied, resting her hands on his arms.

She allowed herself to be pulled into one last embrace, resting her head on his chest and sinking into the warmth of his body for a second. Then she pushed away.

"Atramen is still out there. I must deal with him. I will be back." She kissed him briefly but with passion and then turned and flung herself off the platform. Her body blazed with light and then was gone.

****

Alecyn stepped out of the light into a shadowed decaying stone precinct. Pillars rose from amid moss and weeds on either side of her. Broken marble lay underfoot. A thick, cloying mist clung to her ankles and hid the furthest distance. The air was cold and thin. Ahead of her, along the colonnade of pillars, rose a stone structure. She could make out a tall doorway, black and impenetrable.

Turning, she saw broad stone steps descending into a vertiginous chasm. This place was not a conjuring of the Spirit Road. She was physically here, high in the mountains. This place was the Temple of Ishein, which Atramen had made his hiding place.

She knew how to travel through the rift that Atramen had created and follow the trail of his magic to this place. She had deliberately put aside conscious thought, letting her subconscious take over. The answers were there.

The knowledge rose from the depths of her mind. Now, her shining skin had become crystalline, hardening itself as if preparing to protect her. The Fragment had shaped itself into a sword she clutched in one hand. She did not know how to wield a sword but sensed instinctively that it did not matter. The Fragment had responded to her by shaping itself into a weapon. It would guide her in its use.

"Atramen!" she called out. Her voice rippled the mist, dispersing it in places and driving it back in other waves. "I am here for you! Your army is lost. Your human allies will join us now that you no longer have your Mutes. It is over!"

A ray of sunshine broke through to fall upon her. It glittered off the blade she held. With a wordless cry, a figure came out of the shadows between pillars. He wore figure-hugging leather torn in several places, revealing yellowing flesh beneath. The metal mask broke in two, with one half still clinging in place but ending jaggedly. The skin on his bald scalp looked as thin and brittle as parchment, stretched tightly across it. Around the mouth, it had torn, revealing a permanent grinning skull rictus beneath.

He struck Alecyn with Noise. He hurled a small bulging bag that burst open in contact with the ground. From it came the sounds of pure hell. Pillars shuddered, cracked, and fell. The ground heaved as he flung more of the bags. Noise swirled around Alecyn. It should have been powerful enough to pulverize her flesh. She lifted her sword, and a pure, ringing tone came from it. It dimmed the Noise instantly.

She struck the blade against the ground, and the ground became still where it touched. Atramen opened a music box attached to his belt, pointing it at Alecyn. It sang as she swirled the sword in a circle. It was another ringing tone, but it was light and pure against the pain-soaked chaos of the blood music. The box shattered in Atramen's hands, and he collapsed against a pillar. Alecyn advanced. As she did, he held up his arm and raked his fingers down it. Skin and flesh tore, and the scream from him caused the stone floor to become a powder between him and Alecyn. Again, the music of the blade stilled the chaos.

Alecyn was now a few steps away from him. He cowered before her.

"Please! Please, do not kill me. I will give you my Fragment. Take it!"

He gestured, and a glow appeared from within the dark doorway at the end of the colonnade. It shone gold as a rough-edged metal rectangle flew out the door between the still-standing pillars. Darkness coalesced between Alecyn and the object, and a hand caught the golden tablet from it. The darkness formed itself into a female shape.

The Black Hand suddenly stood before them, holding aloft the Fragment triumphantly.

"You lose, True Voice!" she said mockingly. "This belongs to my master. He will soon have the Fragment belonging to the humans of Welcome, and then the world will tremble before the name Kragen Onyx!"

Alecyn looked at her calmly. "Give me the fragment, Rose. I will destroy you before I let it fall into Onyx's hands."

Rose threw back her head and laughed. "I think not. You may be powerful. But you are no killer. Strike me down. That is the only way you will stop me!"

She tore away the armor at her chest and spread her arms wide. Her eyes glittered with malice, and her smile was pure triumph. "That is why I will always win. "

Another shape coalesced out of the darkness. The shape of the white light was shorter than Rose's but human in form. Alecyn was aware of her Song before she had appeared. It had presaged her arrival like a trumpet blast, but the Black Hand had been so certain of her victory that she had not heard. Eevee took shape behind Rose. The blade she held was real. As Rose whirled around, Eevee was already moving forward. The sword penetrated Rose's chest, slicing through her flesh like a knife through butter. When Eevee pulled it back, there was sadness in her eyes. Rose fell to her knees, blood gushing from the wound. The Fragment fell from her hand.

"Alecyn could never bring herself to kill. Her Waeferen side would have no problem swatting an irritating little insect like you. But her human side would never do it. I am half Waeferen... half cat." Eevee leaned in close. "So, I actually like it," she said with an evil grin, raising the sword again.

"No, Eevee! Don't you dare!" Alecyn commanded. Eevee stayed her hand.

"Go back to your master, Rose. Or stay here and let me cleanse you of his taint. I can do it."

Rose looked up, one hand cupping her escaping lifeblood, and then her body was fading to shadow and dust. She was gone.

"I hope you don't live to regret that girl," Eevee grumbled. She threw the sword away from herself in disgust.

At that moment, Atramen scrabbled for the discarded Song Fragment.

Alecyn was quicker, though. The Fragment lifted from where it lay and floated through the air into her waiting hand. Atramen regained his feet and began to run, sobbing and whimpering, towards the steps.

"Wait!" Alecyn called. "I did not come here to kill you. I meant what I said to Rose. I can heal the taint which has twisted you so."

"Can you, girl?" Eevee muttered, following Alecyn as she advanced after Atramen.

"Let me help you. It is all over now. Your army is gone. Your city is free. It is just you now alone. But it doesn't have to be."

Atramen stopped where the ancient stone stairs curved to follow the mountainside. He laughed and pulled himself upright.

"There is only one end. Without the power you have denied me, there is no life."

He stepped off the step and fell. Alecyn made to lunge after him, but Eevee caught her arm in a vice-like grip.

"Let him die if that is what he wants. It is the least he deserves," she said. "If you won't do it and you won't let me, do it, then let him do it."

Alecyn didn't resist. She walked to the spot from which Atramen had jumped. Somewhere, far below, she could see a tiny, broken figure of a man.

"It's over." Alecyn breathed.

CHAPTER 27:
COMING BACK TO ARGENT

The soft kiss of sunlight in her eyes awoke Alecyn. She stretched languidly and absently reached across to tickle Eevee, where she lay in feline form on the other side of the bed. Alecyn opened her eyes, looking up at the broken mural that had once covered the high ceiling. There hadn't yet been time for cosmetic repairs to Argent. Statues, mosaics, malice, and time had ruined buildings of great majesty and beauty. There hadn't been time to return Argent to its former beauty. The priority was finding homes for everyone, as well as food and clothing. The list went on.

She and Jerad had made their residence in a house that had belonged to a merchant. It stood on a hillside overlooking the harbor, nestled within its own gardens. The people they had brought back to Argent had made them regents. Jerad was reluctant to accept a title, and Alecyn was uncomfortable with ideas like queenship. They had settled for Regent. The palace was, for the moment, uninhabitable and sealed. Too much evil had occurred there. Too much suffering. Alecyn felt the evil of the place the moment she set foot back in the city. So, they had a house that Alecyn loved dearly.

She threw back the bedclothes and walked to the window. From the window, she could see a courtyard where Jerad was already dressed and working. He was talking earnestly to a group of tall, young-looking men. All of Argent's new residents were young-looking. In restoring their humanity, Alecyn had also restored their youth. They gathered around a table that had diagrams and building plans spread out on it. It was the task that had occupied Argent's new residents for the three months since they had returned to the city. Rebuilding. Her own work revolved around the Song Fragment and the Gateway. With Mendel's help, she had opened the Gateway, though the secret of travel between worlds was still beyond her.

But the two of them had directed it to a location within Jonrah. The newly restored people of Argent had returned to their homes through the Gateway while Alecyn, Mendel, and Jerad endured a long stormbird flight. Mendel discovered the secret of locking the Gateway open and in one location, and it now provided a permanent link between Fearnot and Argent.

She watched Jerad for a long moment.

"Out of interest. Have you given any thought to going home?" Eevee asked.

"I am home," Alecyn replied.

"And him?" Eevee pressed as she joined Alecyn at the window. She had transformed into human form, resting her folded arms on the window ledge.

As if sensing his watchers, Jerad looked up from his work. His eyes found Alecyn's, and he smiled. She felt herself blushing, but she didn't look away. She bathed in his attention before a word from one of the young men brought Jerad's attention back.

"He loves me," Alecyn said, aware that she was smiling but unable to stop.

"I can see that. Why do you think I never leave you alone at night?"

Eevee had a mischievous look. "The people want you to be married, you know. I talked to many of them. They all say it. Their great heroic Regents should be wed."

"In time," Alecyn said quietly.

"The two of you won't be able to stay here forever," Eevee said. "Onyx is still out there. And Rose."

Alecyn looked at her. "I am aware of that. Those are dangers for another day. For now. I have earned a rest, at least from fighting. These people need us, Jerad, and I, and you, Eevee. You are too. And Mendel, Idrasi, and the other survivors. This is going to be a place of peace and learning. It is going to be a beacon of hope for all."

"Why set your sights so low, girl? Have some ambition." Eevee said wryly. Alecyn laughed.

"Come on, there's work to be done."

APPENDIX A:
ABOUT THE CHARACTERS

Ademar Montarle

A nobility of Skylands who swore allegiance to the Silence and helped betray his city. It became Nameless. Ademar lusted after power and became a Shrieker in his pursuit of it. He had always taken pleasure in the pain and suffering of others, and Kragen Onyx offered him a way of using that as a source of power. He felt frustrated when the Black Hand made him subordinate, thinking he should have been given the rule of Nameless.

He betrayed Onyx by joining Atramen's rebellion and helping capture the city of Argent. There, he schemed and plotted to find the Song Fragment that Atramen possessed, but he could not uncover its well-hidden location. When Atramen launched his invasion of the Southlands, they gave Ademar command of a portion of his forces.

Alecyn Johnsenn

A nurse from Lake Wales, Florida. A sinkhole swallows her home while she sleeps, within which is a gateway to the world of Jonrah. In Jonrah, Alecyn has the power of a Singer, the ability to work magic through music and the True Voice and fulfill an ancient prophecy sung by the Wayfarer race and kept alive by humans and Nelim. This prophecy concerns a human who can cleanse the Great Song, the power that drives the universe, from the corruption inflicted by the Silence.

Alyssa Palene

Former wife to Jerad, Singer to the Argent royal court and a Harmony member. Alyssa had devoted her life to a study of the Wayfarer prophecies and the gateways. It was Alyssa who first found Rose Blackwell and discovered Altraman's betrayal. He murdered her and stole her life's work. Many believe that this work contains fragments of the Great Song, which was long believed to be lost when Onyx attempted to change it.

Aoife

Singer to the town of Fearnot. Wife of the town blacksmith, Harl. Aoife has some ability as a healer and player of the Harp, the instrument maintained by the community for the town's benefit. When Alecyn destroys the Veil over the city of Argent, Aoife receives knowledge of it through the Spirit Road, and her warnings prompt Jerad to go to Argent to rescue the woman she believes to be the True Voice.

Atramen

Once a powerful human Singer who fought against the Silence. Atramen was a member of the Harmony, a group of the most powerful Singers and Players across the races. He betrayed the Harmony, leading a group of young human Singers in an uprising in Welcome. They murdered many of their former friends and fellow Harmony members and took secrets and artifacts of power over to the Silence. Atramen's betrayal led to the capture of Rose Blackwell as the Harmony tried to bring her from Earth to a secure Gateway protected by Erevar the Eternal.

Atramen turned her to the Silence, and then together, they broke the human and Nelim forces that tried to rescue her from Satan's Kingdom in the War of the Broken Strings. By the end of the war, the Harmony broke, dividing humans and Nelim, and Atramen claimed the human city of Argent as his domain.

Avery

A member of the town council of Fearnot. He is the head law enforcement official. Although there is not much conflict in Fearnot, he ensures the citizens know their responsibilities and what they can and cannot do. He also works to get new citizens acclimated to the ways of Fearnot.

Eevee

Alecyn's cat travels to Jonrah with her through the sinkhole/ gateway. In Jonrah Eevee begins to change...

Erevar

A Nelim mystic and Player who controls a gateway and is one of the last surviving members of the Harmony. His origins are unknown, though Nelim legends tell of a drum player named Erevar the Thunder, fighting a duel against Kragen Onyx and dealing him with a great injury during the Great War of the Song. His name appears scattered throughout stories and songs, with little known for certain. The Nelim Book of the Forest, the history of their race, contains an account of a powerful Player who gave his life in defense of the Nelim settlement of Canopy (subsequently destroyed utterly) during the Great War of the Song. The account tells of his single-handedly holding off the forces of the Silence while the Nelim escaped the city and how he later died of his wounds. Subsequently, Alecyn encountered a mystic named Erevar within the Heart, who guided her on her journey.

Jerad Palene

Leader of the community of Fearnot in the Southlands. Formerly, Jerad served in the Resounding Guards, the elite regiment of Argent, and was husband to Alyssa. After his wife's death and the city's fall, he gathered the survivors of the Resounding Guard and fought against Atramen until only he remained. Jerad and the remaining Guards earned a fearsome reputation for their remorseless fight and limitless brutality against any who supported Atramen. They terrorized Atramen's creatures and allies throughout the Northlands until they were eventually defeated, leaving only their leader alive. Subsequently, he wandered the wilderness between the northlands and the south until the community of Fearnot took him in.

Hayden

A member of the town council of Fearnot and Jerad's second-hand man. He sees the city's day-to-day operations.

Kragen Onyx

A human Singer, the greatest the world has ever seen. He tried to improve the Great Song but could not match the perfection of its Creator. Instead, the song was corrupted, leading to war between humanity and the other races of Jonrah. The war caused the lands of Jonrah to be shattered and reshaped, and it remade and scattered its people. The Wayfarers made gateways and used them to escape the war. Onyx became known as the Silence and took control of an island known as Satan's Kingdom. He fights to control the gateways and the Great Song.

Krissker

A Kajani of Greyfoot Pride, Dancing Waters den. Krissker and his brothers became orphans after a pride war between the Greyfoots and the Sunmanes. As darkness spread across Jonrah and greater enemies rose, Krissker and the Greyfoot Pride stood beside Jerad and the True Voice, not as followers, but as equals. He became a bridge between old instincts and new purpose. A warrior who proved that even those born from war could choose honor over hatred. Krissker is strength shaped by loss, loyalty carved through hardship, and living proof that the fiercest hearts are not always those that seek battle… but those that survive it, rise above it, and choose who they will fight for.

Lucas Haverford

Storm bird trainer and rider for the town of Fearnot. When Jerad learns the Veil has been broken, he enlists Lucas' help to fly to Argent. Lucas grew up in Ghoul's Creek, where his father was a fisherman. A storm claimed the life of his father and left Lucas stranded on an island off the south coast of Jonrah. A storm bird rescued him and he subsequently discovered an affinity for the giant birds. Lucas met Jerad and was welcomed by the people of Fearnot, where he learned to master his skill in communicating with the stormbirds, training them, and using them for his new community. The people of Ghoul's Creek continue to view him and the stormbirds with suspicion. Still, many of the practical

Southland communities have embraced this innovation, seeking Lucas' help training their own flocks. Through Lucas' ability, the Southlands have become famous for their stormbird riders.

Mendel Alainen

A Nelim of the mystic caste (the Higher caste of Heart society). Mendel is a scholar who is learning under the tutelage of Erevar. He has the lighter blue skin of the forest Nelim, who originated in the lands south of Argent. Pursuing knowledge is paramount to Mendel, as it is to all the mystic castes. Mendel, a pacifist frightened by violence, can show rare courage in defending his beliefs and those he cares for. His study area is the prophecy of the True Voice and the Fragments of the Great Song. Mendel possesses some magical abilities, as do many of the Nelim mystic caste.

Mutes

Creatures brought into existence by Atramen from the captive population of Argent, taken when the Veil trapped them inside the city. Atramen stole their voices to feed his power, and the Shriekers gave them new voices produced from the distilled pain and suffering of their torture victims. These new voices corrupted and transformed the forms of those who received them. Mutes feed on sound of any kind and regurgitate it as a chaotic noise that can debilitate or even kill. Their primary weapon, though, is ingesting the sounds made by any living thing, draining the life force with the sound. Atramen has produced thousands of Mutes.

Rose Blackwell

The first human to be targeted by a sinkhole and pass through the gateway to Jonrah. The Harmony believed her to be the fulfillment of the True Voice prophecy; however, their attempt to reach her failed. Atramen captured her and turned her to the Silence. Known as the Black Hand, she fought for the Silence in the War of Broken Strings and led a force that captured the Human / Nelim city of Skylands. She claimed the city as her own, henceforth known as Nameless. The Black Hand is Silence's most trusted lieutenant and is even more powerful than Atramen.

Shriekers

They were human Singers and Players who went over to the Silence. Their power originates from the world around them, and this power corrodes their humanity and physical form, forcing them to cover and mask themselves. They draw power from pain and suffering, inflicting torture to capture the agonized voices of their victims to be used as a weapon (blood music) or to sustain themselves. They are the eyes and ears of the Silence and Atramen.

Stormbirds

Giant eagles roost in the mountain chain that runs west to east across the eastern half of Jonrah. Humans bred them in ancient times before the Great War of the Song as transportation. Humans and Stormbirds have evolved together, and humankind have a strong affinity for the birds. Following the war, they became wild when their habitats were destroyed, and the world changed. A small number found shelter in the Hasten Mountains, and this colony saved the species from extinction. Humanity has forgotten its affinity for birds. Lucas Haverford found his ability unlocked during his hour of the most desperate need when a stormbird rescued him. From him, modern humans in the Southland have been rediscovering their ability to train and ride the gigantic birds.

From the small number that survived the War of the Song, the stormbird population now numbers in the thousands and is thriving. Southlanders have trained and tamed approximately one hundred in the last decade, and despite his early age, Lucas Haverford manages more trained birds than any other individual.

Vanja Haj'rath

The leader of the Nelim warriors in the Heart. He is tall, even for a Nelim, standing at about seven feet. He has the purple skin of the Farain Nelim, who originated in the far west of Jonrah. They were driven from these lands during the War of the Song. His skin bears tattoos that symbolize his loyalty to the cult of Mithraen, an ancient Nelim God of war. He is the leader of a warrior band of Mithraen worshippers, the Velesten. The mystics led by Erevar, who govern Nelim society in the Heart, dismiss this cult. This has led to Vanja being the center of growing discontent with the rule of the Higher's (the mystic caste who occupies the higher levels of the Heart). Vanja believes Erevar has betrayed the Nelim into hiding from the Silence, thus surrendering their ancestral lands to the humans. He wants to return to Jonrah and fight for it. Vanja is quick to anger and is naturally belligerent towards all but a close number of fellow warriors he respects. He is one of the Nelim's greatest warriors.

Wayfarers

One of the ancient races of Jonrah. During the War of the Song, the Wayfarers created gateways to escape the chaos. The last to travel through the Gateways left a prophecy behind of the coming of the True Voice, a Singer of unprecedented power who will restore the harmony of the Great Song.

ABOUT THE AUTHOR

C. S. Zahn lives with her son in Rutland, VT, and works part-time as an oncology data specialist at the local hospital. Born in Potsdam, New York, her parents moved to Fairless Hills, Pennsylvania, when she was about 2 years old. She has lived in many parts of the country: Connecticut, New York City, Florida, Alaska, and Texas. She has two children, two grandchildren, and two great-grandchildren.

Cindy holds three post-secondary degrees: an associate degree in business administration, a bachelor's degree in organization management, and a Master of Science degree in health services administration. This is the second book in the Land of Jonrah series, which will be at least three books long.

She has enjoyed reading science fiction and fantasy books, which are her favorite genres. Her favorite authors are the late Robert Jordan, L.E. Modesitt, and Terry Goodkind.

"To me, to write a series of books that runs for 13 to 14 books is inspiring."

Visit my website at https.landofjonrah.com. Or you can follow her author Facebook page:

https://www.facebook.com/cszahnauthor.

She also has her own website: www.landofjonrah.com.

Here, you can purchase her books, post comments, get more information on the characters, and find out when the next book will be available.

Thank you for choosing The Resurrection of Jonrah, Book 2 of the Land of Jonrah series. If you enjoyed this story, please leave a review so others can decide if this is a book they like.

www.ingramcontent.com/pod-product-compliance
Lightning Source LLC
LaVergne TN
LVHW030910080826
845145LV00010B/2843

* 9 7 8 1 9 6 2 9 7 3 5 2 6 *